"What did you find down there?"

"Where?"

"At my campsite down by the river. Something's wrong. I can tell."

He shook his head. "Nothing you don't already know about. But I saw what they did to your raft. Vicious, the way they ripped it apart."

"Yes." It was vicious, done by someone with a vicious mind. "I thank God that Keira remembered to use her bear spray and get away from them. But they're gone now. We'll be okay until a rescue party arrives."

"I'll keep you safe." Zeke spoke as if saying the words aloud would make them true.

The dots connected. "That's why you said you'd go fishing with us tomorrow. To keep us safe."

Zeke shrugged and added more wood to the fire under the pot of water Alexis was heating to wash up.

"You don't have to babysit us."

"Maybe not." He met her eyes. "But if anything happened to you or Keira, I wouldn't be able to live with myself."

Beth Carpenter is thankful for good books, a good dog, a good man and a dream job creating happily-ever-afters. She and her husband now split their time between Alaska and Arizona, where she occasionally encounters a moose in the yard or a scorpion in the basement. She prefers the moose.

Books by Beth Carpenter

Harlequin Heartwarming

A Northern Lights Novel

The Alaskan Catch
A Gift for Santa
Alaskan Hideaway
An Alaskan Proposal
Sweet Home Alaska
Alaskan Dreams
An Alaskan Family Christmas
An Alaskan Homecoming

Visit the Author Profile page at Harlequin.com.

Kidnapped
in Alaska

BETH CARPENTER

LOVE INSPIRED
INSPIRATIONAL ROMANCE

LOVE INSPIRED®
INSPIRATIONAL ROMANCE

ISBN-13: 978-1-335-42615-4

Kidnapped in Alaska

Love Inspired
22 Adelaide St. West, 41st Floor
Toronto, Ontario M5H 4E3, Canada
www.LoveInspired.com

Printed in U.S.A.

Are not two sparrows sold for a farthing? and one of them shall not fall on the ground without your Father. But the very hairs of your head are all numbered. Fear ye not therefore, ye are of more value than many sparrows.

—*Matthew* 10:29–31

For my mother, who showed me how to face life with courage, optimism and faith.

Chapter One

"Keira, you can't catch a fish if you don't put your line in the water." Alexis Mahoney suppressed a laugh as her not-quite-teenage niece responded with a Broadway-worthy sigh before returning her precious new cell phone to the pocket of her hiking shorts. Even though they were in the wilds of Alaska, out of reach of any cell tower, Keira insisted on checking the phone at least hourly. Whether from habit or devotion, Alexis wasn't sure.

Poppy, Alexis's Labrador retriever mix, applauded Keira's dramatic performance by thumping her tail against the yellow daisy-printed camp mat where she lay. Poppy had gotten her name when two-year-old Keira hadn't been able to pronounce "puppy," and they'd been pals ever since. Poppy's muzzle sported some gray hairs now, but unlike Keira, she was always up for an adventure.

"I can't believe I don't get to go with my friends

to the indie-band concert on the Anchorage town square tomorrow," Keira huffed as she picked up the rod Alexis had rigged for her. "I've had nothing to do all summer, and when something good finally happens, I have to miss it."

"I know." Alexis was disappointed, too, not about the concert, since despite Keira's claim, she'd attended several already this summer, but in her brother, Dixon. The mother of one of Keira's friends had arranged with Dixon to take the two girls and several of their friends to the concert together. Keira would never say it aloud, but Alexis knew it had meant a lot to her that her father would be there. Except he'd canceled. Again.

Still, the situation wasn't as bad as Keira made it out to be. Alexis had planned this entire fly-in float trip to make up for Dixon's absence, and it wasn't as though Keira had been confined to her room for the last three months. "You went with Elise's family to the jazz concert at Bear Tooth Theatre in June, and I took you, Elise and Sarah to a concert at the PAC two weeks ago."

"Those were boring." Keira indulged in an eye roll before throwing out a half-hearted cast.

"Oh, really?" At the concert, Keira and her two best friends had gushed about the music. Keira must have changed her mind based on a thumbs-down from one of the popular kids in her class. Alexis could remember a few angsty teenage days of her own, obsessing over the opinions of people she didn't even like.

Fortunately for her, that phase had ended quickly after Alexis's father, on a raft trip much like this one, had made her understand there were no winners in that game. Alexis hoped to impart the same wisdom to Keira before she tied herself into knots, always trying to land on the right side of cool. Assuming *cool* still meant *cool*.

Keira's only reply was a disdainful shrug as she moved farther up the bank, away from Alexis.

Of course, one could hardly blame Keira for being image-conscious, considering her mother collected status symbols like souvenir postcards. When Alexis had picked up Keira for the trip yesterday, she'd noticed Mara's silver BMW had been replaced with a black Range Rover still sporting temporary license plates. Meanwhile, Dixon had gotten so wrapped up in running Mahoney Tours he never seemed to find a spare moment for his daughter.

Keira was, in fact, supposed to be spending the next two weeks with Dixon, according to their visitation agreement, but some business emergency had sent him flying off to Ketchikan and then Juneau with an urgent plea for Alexis to take her niece for the first week. That was when Alexis had come up with the idea for a rafting trip, just the two of them, although it had taken a major bribe from Dixon to sell the plan to Keira. Thus the new cell phone, which, since Alexis didn't intend to tell Keira about the solar charger she'd brought along, would shortly turn into an expensive paperweight for the duration of the trip.

Alexis cast out her fly line, skillfully settling the fly at the edge of a shady pool on the far side of the river where she hoped a silver salmon or two might be resting from their upstream migration. No takers yet. The main run wasn't due for two weeks or so, which was why she and Keira had the river to themselves right now, but there were always a few salmon ahead of the curve. Alexis had brought along a second fly rod and waders, thinking she might give Keira her first lessons in fly-fishing, but considering Keira's mood, Alexis chose to let her continue to fish from the bank with a familiar spinning reel. Fly-fishing took patience. Teaching someone fly-fishing took even more, and Alexis was beginning to suspect the next six days could use up all her reserves.

Something rustled in the woods on the other side of the river. Something large. Keira froze, her eyes wide. "Bear?"

Alexis peered into the trees, but she couldn't make out any shapes. "Maybe. I haven't seen any sign, but anytime you find salmon, you might find bears." The rustle sounded again, slightly upstream of where it was before. It could be a bear, but the noise wasn't quite right. Could be a person, but the fly-in service that dropped them at Pearson Lake had mentioned they had no other paddlers scheduled on the river this week.

However, the river here was deep enough for someone in a powerboat from Pearson Lake to have made their way down. The breeze blew upstream, so she and Keira might not have heard the motor. If this was one of the residents from the cabins at the lake, surely they would step out and make themselves known. Poppy didn't seem to notice anything amiss, but then Poppy's hearing wasn't what it used to be.

"Great. I miss the concert so I can get eaten by a bear," Keira grumbled as she reeled in her line. "Totally worth it."

"You'll be fine. Generally, if you leave bears alone, they'll leave you alone. But I'm armed, just in case." Alexis touched the .44 Magnum in the holster on her hip, a practical gun, powerful enough to stop a bear if necessary but small enough to carry while she fished. "You've got your bear spray, right?"

"Of course." Keira nodded at the canister on her belt.

"Good. Don't go anywhere without it."

"I know." Keira pulled back her rod and cast the pixie lure, apparently over her bear scare.

Alexis watched the far bank for a few more minutes but nothing appeared. She heard only the usual sounds of birdsong and rushing water. It was probably just a squirrel. It was amazing how much noise the little critters could make scurrying around dry leaves. She gathered up her line and was about to cast again when she saw Keira's line jog upstream. "Keira! You've got a bite! Set the hook!"

Keira whooped, giving Alexis a glimpse of the little girl who used to love fishing and had longed for the days when she was old enough for a rafting trip like this. She jerked the rod upward and began reeling in the fish, keeping her tip up just the way Alexis had taught her. "I think it's a big one!"

"Good, because I'm hungry." Alexis waded closer to the bank, net at the ready. Poppy eased nearer but stayed out of the way. As the fish thrashed in the shallows, pink spots on a darker background came into view, along with a reddish blush along the belly. "Ooh, you've got a Dolly Varden."

"Oh, wow! I've never caught a Dolly before." Keira guided the fish closer, where Alexis could net it. A few minutes later, Alexis used the last of the battery on Keira's cell phone to capture a photo of Keira, dark eyes sparkling, with her first Dolly.

"It's a beauty. I'll clean it if you'll get the fire ready and put on two skillets."

"Deal." By the time Alexis had cleaned and filleted the fish, Keira had the coals from that morning's fire raked together under a grate supporting two cast-iron skillets. Alexis collected the cedar plank she'd left soaking in water, arranged one of the fillets on top, and seasoned it with her own special spice mix and a squeeze of lemon. While the skillets heated, she chopped up potato, bell pepper and onion.

She set the damp plank on the grill and turned one of the hot skillets upside down to cover it. Leaving the fish to cook, she sautéed the vegetables in a little oil in the second skillet. Back when she used to work summers for her dad as a river guide, this meal was always a client favorite. Ten minutes later, she seasoned the vegetables with salt and pepper and slid them and the fish onto plates.

She and Keira settled into folding chairs. Alexis bowed her head. "Thank You, God, for providing us with this bounty. Bless the hands that prepared the food and the girl who caught the fish. Amen."

"Amen," Keira echoed and dug in.

Alexis took her first bite. Perfect. Nothing beat fresh fish, right out of the river. Poppy, knowing Alexis's rules about begging, strategically situated herself next to Keira. Keira slipped her a nugget of her fish, and Alexis pretended not to see. Keira took another bite of fish and eagerly scooped up more vegetables. "These potatoes are so good. Mom's on a diet and we can't have any carbs in the house. I miss spaghetti."

"I'll bet." Keira, in the middle of a growth spurt, had the long-limbed look of a fawn and the appetite of a lumberjack. In the past year, she'd grown to within a few inches of Alexis's five-six. Mara was probably cutting back on calories now so that she could indulge on the European cruise she'd scheduled to take during the two weeks Keira was supposed to spend with Dixon. "When does your mom leave for Barcelona?"

"Oh, she's not going. She says she can't afford it

after she bought a new car, but she lost her cruise deposit when she canceled. She's been griping about it all week."

"That's too bad." Mara was never easy to live with when she was feeling deprived. And it seemed to happen a lot.

Alexis and Dixon's father, founder of Mahoney Tours, had died suddenly when Alexis was a sophomore in college, four years after their mother had passed. Dixon, who at twenty-five had been working with their dad for three years, had stepped forward to take over the firm. Shortly afterward, he and Mara divorced, and at her request, he'd borrowed the money to buy out Mara rather than give her partial ownership in Mahoney Tours. He'd bought out the shares Alexis had inherited as well, which had provided the money she needed to finish college and later to start her own engineering consulting company.

Since that time, Dixon had expanded Mahoney Tours from a small adventure tour company to a huge business with its own lodges, buses and even a ski resort. In the process, he had made himself a tidy fortune, and Mara resented it. His ex-wife had a habit of complaining to anyone who would listen that she'd been cheated out of her rightful share of the business.

Alexis didn't see it that way. Dixon had paid them each a fair price for her share of the company as it had existed at the time. The company's growth afterward was due to his own talent and hard work, but it came at a price. His ex-wife despised him, and he barely knew his daughter. Alexis much preferred her own business in structural-design consulting. It wouldn't make her rich, but it allowed her a comfortable living doing work she loved, with time off for the important things. Hiking with friends. Throwing balls for the dog. Church activities. And most importantly, spending time with her niece.

Keira scraped up the final bite from the plate. "Any more of that left?" Her mood had improved considerably. Maybe she'd been cranky because she was hungry.

"Help yourself from the skillet over there."

Keira hopped up and filled her plate. "Do you want more?"

"No, thanks. You can have the rest."

After devouring most of her second helping, Keira set her fork down. "Dad says there's white water on this float."

"That's right. We'll be hitting some smaller rapids on our next float day, and at the end of the trip the narrows just above Chapel Lake are class three."

Keira's eyes lit up. "Class three? Cool. Dad never let me do white water before."

"Well, now you will. Do you want to take a hike later? There's a waterfall not too far from here that's supposed to be spectacular. The sun doesn't set until ten thirty tonight, so we have plenty of time."

Keira looked up from her plate. "You've never

seen the waterfall?" She knew Alexis and Dixon used to lead rafting tours down this river every summer.

"No." Alexis grinned. "When we were guiding together, your dad was in charge. He always took the clients hiking and left me behind to cook dinner."

Keira laughed. "He still hates to cook. He knows all the pizza delivery people by their first names."

"Well, fortunately I like to cook, since there's no pizza delivery out here." Alexis got up to give the last few scraps on her plate to Poppy. "We need to wash the dishes and cache our food between trees so we don't draw bears into camp. Then we can take the trail to Leah Falls and see if it's as amazing as they say."

"Okay." Keira finished her last bite of potato. "As long as we're back in time for dinner."

The hike to the waterfall hadn't looked that long on a map, but it turned out to be a steeper trail than Alexis had anticipated. By the time they reached the tree line, Keira was huffing and puffing, but she still found the breath to whine, "The mosquitoes are eating me up."

"Here. Use more of this." Alexis pulled a bottle of heavy-duty insect repellent from her pack and squirted some on Keira's hands. Alaskans joked that although the willow ptarmigan was the official state bird, it should really be the mosquito.

Once she'd rubbed more repellent on her arms and neck, Keira collapsed onto a boulder in the alpine meadow. "Where is this waterfall, anyway? The North Pole?" Poppy came to rest her head against Keira's leg, and Keira rubbed her ears.

"It should be close," Alexis answered after studying the map she'd preloaded onto her phone. "I'll tell you what. You rest for a minute. I'll climb to the top of this hill and see if I can see Leah Falls from there."

"Fine." Keira pulled her water bottle from her day pack and took a drink.

Alexis headed up the trail. Clusters of bright pink fireweed almost as tall as she was lined the edges of the trail. Now that they were out of the trees, she could see Denali in the distance, just the peak rising above the clouds clinging to the sides of the mountain. She climbed higher and spotted what looked like a lowbush blueberry patch not far from the trail. It was about the right time of year for the berries to ripen. Once they'd seen Leah Falls, she'd have to take Keira over to see if there were any ready to pick.

She scrambled up a steep chute between boulders and reached the top of the pass. Sure enough, across the valley, Leah Falls tumbled down the mountain in lacy tiers like a bridal veil. Beyond it, snowcapped mountains reached for the clouds in the sky. The view was so spectacular, Alexis was inspired to just stop and be in awe of God's creation for a moment. She could hardly wait to share it with Keira.

She turned and had started back down the trail when she heard a scream, followed by Poppy's barking. Not her "chasing a squirrel" bark but a deep, frantic warning. Alexis slid down the chute and scrambled between the boulders until she could see the meadow where she'd left Keira. Instead of sitting peacefully on the rock, Keira was in the middle of the field, struggling against a man who had her by the arm.

"Stop it!" Alexis yelled as she plunged down the mountain, risking a tumble. "Let her go!"

The man ignored Alexis's shout and continued pulling Keira toward the woods. He wore a green baseball cap and a buff covered his face up to his sunglasses. Poppy barked and growled, circling the man, but she couldn't seem to stop him. Alexis caught a flash of orange from between trees at the edge of the meadow. Another man? She continued running toward them. She had her gun, but she certainly wasn't going to point it at Keira. *God, please keep her safe!*

Suddenly, the man released Keira and fell back, cursing, his hands covering his face. Keira jumped away, still holding the can of bear spray she'd used on him. *Smart girl!* She turned and ran toward Alexis. The man stumbled forward, still clutching his eyes, but he stumbled over the dog, which gave Keira a good head start. By the time Keira reached Alexis, Poppy had caught up and was at her heels. The man who'd tried to drag her into the woods didn't seem to be armed, but the second one could be. Alexis wasn't going to take that risk. "Come on. We need to get out of here."

Alexis led the way across the brow of the hill, running as fast as she dared. It left them exposed if the other man decided to shoot, but it ran above the upper reaches of a ravine that would hopefully block the men from taking the angle and cutting them off. Behind them, she heard shouts and footsteps, but she didn't slow down to look back. Once she, Keira and Poppy were on the other side of the ravine, she dropped them down to the woods, skirting the edges until she spotted a game trail they could follow without crashing through the brush. After they were in the woods hidden from view, she stopped and turned to Keira. "Are you okay?"

Keira nodded, her hands on her knees while she gasped for breath. "Are—are they still coming?"

"I don't know." Alexis couldn't see them, but she thought she heard voices. "Can you run farther?"

"Yes."

"Okay, let's go." The more distance they could put between themselves and the two men, the better. Alexis took off again, careful to keep the mountain peaks to their right. She kept her pace to one Keira could maintain along the winding game trails. Keira resolutely followed, with Poppy close behind. They crossed a couple of narrow creeks and scrambled over a few scree piles along the way. Alexis wasn't sure how far they'd gone, but it felt like they'd been running for hours when Keira tripped on a root and went down. Hard.

Alexis dropped beside her. "Ouch! That had to hurt."

Keira sucked in a breath through her teeth. "Just my knee." She rolled into a sitting position, holding the skinned knee, and Alexis realized her eyes were irritated and running with tears. Some of the bear spray must have blown back toward her face. How had she made it this far without tripping?

Alexis took her water bottle from her day pack and passed it to Keira. "Here. Try to rinse your eyes."

Keira did, pouring some of the water over her face and then drinking deeply. "That feels a little better."

"Good." Alexis unzipped her backpack and found an antiseptic wipe in her portable first aid kit. "This knee doesn't look too bad. Does it hurt a lot?" She dabbed it with the wipe.

"Not until you did that! Ouch!" Keira was starting to sound like herself again. "That stings."

"I know, and I'm sorry. I'm almost done." She finished cleaning the scrape and covered it with a clean bandage. "There." She paused for a minute, listening, but didn't hear any shouts or footsteps. "I think we lost them." She grinned at Keira. "Using your bear spray on that guy—you're brilliant!"

"Yeah, yeah. I know." Keira grinned back. Poppy crowded in to give Keira a lick on the cheek in solidarity. Keira put her arms around the dog and hugged her.

Alexis stood and walked a few steps down the trail. Now what? They needed to get back to camp and move on down the river away from the men who had threatened Keira, but Alexis wasn't sure exactly where they were now. She closed her eyes. *Lord, I need help. I have to keep Keira safe. Please show me the way.*

Okay. Time to take stock. She couldn't call for help because she'd left her satellite phone back at camp, thinking they'd only be hiking for two hours and not wanting to carry the extra half pound. Bad move on her part. Not that anyone would be able to reach them for hours anyway, but it would be nice to know backup was coming. She did have her cell phone with her, though, and she'd downloaded trail maps of the area before they'd left. She pulled the phone from her pocket.

Keira eyed her suspiciously. "I thought there were no cell towers out here."

"There aren't. But if we can get a clear shot at the sky, we should be able to pick up GPS." She checked the map. Even without knowing exactly where they were, she could see that Leah Falls was the only marked trail in the entire area. She certainly wasn't taking Keira back to the waterfall trail where the men had attacked her, but the map showed several creeks coming down the mountain, fed by the snow-fields up top. If they could find a creek, they could follow it to the river and then follow the river back to their campsite. "We need to go uphill above the tree line and see if I can pick up satellite signals." Alexis offered a hand up.

Keira climbed to her feet. Her eyes weren't tearing any longer, but they were still red and swollen.

She took a tentative step, limping just a bit, and then looked up at Alexis. "What are we waiting for? Let's go."

Alexis gave her niece a hug. "You are the strongest, bravest girl in the whole world. You know that, right?"

"If you say so." Keira laughed. "Come on. Let's get moving."

They moved slowly but steadily uphill until they'd reached another alpine meadow. Keira sat down to rest, while Alexis worked her phone. After a bit, an indicator popped up on the map, pinpointing their location. Alexis showed it to Keira. "See, we're right here. And these are our coordinates."

"Does my phone do this?" Keira asked.

"Sure. Although since you're off-line and didn't download any maps, it would just show you the indicator and the coordinates." She pointed to the southeast. "Looks like if we continue in that direction, we should hit a creek, and then we can follow it down to the river and back to camp."

"And then what?" Keira asked. Alexis could tell she was trying to be brave, but her voice trembled a little.

Alexis tried to project confidence. "Then I'll use my sat phone to call and report those men, and we'll pack up camp and move downriver far away from them. We'll let the troopers handle it from there. Okay?"

"Okay." Keira ran a hand over Poppy's head, got to her feet and limped toward Alexis. "Let's go."

Chapter Two

Two hours later, Keira's limp had become more pronounced, and they still hadn't found the creek. Alexis stopped and pulled two energy bars from her pack. "Hungry?"

"Kinda." Keira sat down, unwrapped her bar and took a bite. Alexis started to follow suit, but after thinking about it, she returned the bar to her pack. Keira might need it more later. When Keira finished her bar, Alexis gave her the last swallow from her water bottle. Keira's was missing, presumably dropped in the struggle.

From the map on her phone, they should be close enough to touch the creek, but she still hadn't seen a sign of it. Which made her question the accuracy of the map and GPS. The wind shifted and with it came a welcome sound. *Thank You, God!* "Keira, do you hear that? Water!"

"Good. I'm still thirsty."

"Oh, um, sorry, but you can't drink water from a creek without treating it. It could make you really sick." And their high-tech filter and UV water purifier were back at camp, of course. From now on, Alexis wasn't leaving camp without a packet of water purification tablets in her first aid kit. Assuming she made it back to restock the kit. "Come on, kid. Once we find the creek, we can follow it to the river and find our camp."

"Is it a long way?" Keira asked in a small voice.

"Not far, and it's all downhill." *Not far* might be stretching the truth, but she had to give Keira hope. She wasn't going to leave a twelve-year-old here in the woods by herself while she went in search of their food and equipment. She needed Keira to believe she could do it. "God will get us through this."

Keira searched Alexis's face. "You really believe that?"

"I really do." She offered a hand. After a moment's hesitation, Keira gave a little smile and let Alexis pull her to her feet. Just past the next bend in the trail, they saw a creek tumbling down the mountain. A well-used game trail ran parallel to the edge of the creek. If the terrain didn't get too steep, Keira should be able to manage it.

The trail became wider as they descended. Keira followed gamely, but she began to lag. Alexis stopped to let her catch up. Keira looked longingly at the water. "Are you sure we can't drink it? It looks clean."

Alexis shook her head, although her throat felt

parched, too. "You can't see the amoebas, but they're probably there, especially if there are any beavers living upstream. We'll get you all the water you want once we get back to camp."

"Okay." Keira started forward. They'd been following the creek for a half hour or so when the unmistakable thwack of an axe hitting wood reached Alexis's ears. Keira heard it, too, and let out a little whimper of fear. Could it be the men from earlier? The sound seemed to be coming from a spot directly in their path. Alexis swallowed.

"You stay here and keep Poppy with you," she whispered. "I'll slip down and check it out."

"Don't leave me," Keira begged.

"I just want to make sure it's safe first."

"But what if you don't come back? I can't—" A small sob escaped.

"Shh, it's okay." Alexis gave her a hug. "We'll go together. But we need to be quiet." Alexis turned to the dog. "Poppy, stay."

Poppy's brown eyes were filled with reproach at being left behind, but the dog remained in a sit/stay while Alexis and Keira crept forward. As they came to the edge of the woods, a log cabin came into view. Actually, only a partially completed cabin, with the logs stacked to head height, blocking their view of whoever was using the axe.

Alexis put her finger to her lips and tilted her head, signaling to Keira that they should stay in the trees and circle around until they could see the action. Another cabin, this one complete but only about twelve feet square, was located behind and to the side of the bigger cabin. The small one appeared windowless except for a high opening just under the eaves. Maybe a storage building? A few wildflowers bloomed on the sod roof, beside a galvanized stovepipe. A matching log outhouse stood a little distance downhill. Between the two cabins, a cast-iron Dutch oven balanced on three flat rocks. Embers glowed from the low fire underneath.

In the center of the clearing was the source of the noise, a man stripping the limbs from a downed tree. He raised his axe and with one blow removed the last branch. He dragged the branch to a pile at the edge of the clearing and returned to the log, where he picked up a two-handed tool and went to work stripping the bark. He wore heavy boots, canvas work pants and a flannel shirt. His bushy brown beard was a shade lighter than his hair, which he'd tied back away from his face. There didn't appear to be anyone else around.

Staying in the shadows, Alexis and Keira moved back behind the main cabin where they could remain out of his sight. "What do you think?" Alexis whispered. "Could he be one of the men from the Leah Falls Trail?"

"Men?" Keira whispered back. "I only saw one."

"He had a partner. I saw someone with orange shoes in the woods."

Keira thought for a moment. "The man who grabbed

me was wearing blue jeans and a black T-shirt, and he was wearing a buff over his face, but I don't think he had a beard underneath. This guy has khaki pants and a flannel shirt. And brown boots."

"And judging by the pile of limbs, it looks like he's been working all day," Alexis mused. Keira licked her lips, dry and cracked. She needed water and rest. Alexis closed her eyes. *Lord, can we trust him?*

At a rustling sound behind them, they turned. Poppy must have decided they'd abandoned her. When she spotted them, she gave a bark of joy and came galloping over, tail wagging madly, as though they'd been gone for days rather than minutes.

"Hush, Poppy." Alexis crouched down and ran a hand over the smooth blond head, trying to settle the dog.

"Do you think that guy's a hermit, all by himself out here?" Keira asked in a stage whisper. "Maybe he, like, hates other people and is sworn to be alone all the time."

"Shh. We don't want him to hear us."

Too late. The man stepped around to the side of the cabin, still holding the axe. He raised a hand to shade his face. "Who's there?" His voice was husky, as though he wasn't used to speaking aloud.

The decision taken out of her hands, Alexis stood and offered a friendly smile. "Hi. Just two hikers and a dog passing by. I wonder if we could trouble you for some treated water to drink."

Wary eyes swept over them, momentarily resting

on the gun on Alexis's hip and then moving on to Keira. "Where did you come from?"

Poppy wagged her tail at the sound of his voice. Alexis would have liked to trust in Poppy's character evaluation, but except for her unfounded hatred of the postal carrier and her protective reaction against Keira's attacker, the Labrador had always been notoriously friendly. Alexis moved a step closer to Keira. "We were hiking and got a little off the trail. If you could just spare a drink and let me refill my water bottle, we'll get out of your hair and head on back to camp."

"You mean the Leah Falls Trail?" At Alexis's nod, he tilted his head and took a step closer. "That's three miles from here."

It was disheartening to hear they'd only traveled three miles in all those hours, but with all the winding trails and moving up and down the mountain, Alexis could believe it. Besides, that meant they were closer to camp than she'd originally thought. "We had a little incident."

"I see." He scowled. "And you only brought one water bottle for the two of you? Did you bring food? Jackets? Matches?"

They did have jackets, matches and one remaining energy bar, and they'd started out with plenty of water for a two-hour hike. Alexis's first impulse was to explain what had happened to Keira, but what if this man was a friend of the other two? Besides, she didn't owe him an explanation. Instead of answering, she took a cue from Keira and simply shrugged.

He stared at them for a moment longer, but Alexis thought she could see his eyes soften as he noticed the bandage on Keira's knee. Poppy walked over to him and nuzzled his hand. Almost as a reflex, he scratched behind the dog's ears. "All right, then. Come with me and I'll get you something to drink." He turned abruptly and started toward the smaller cabin with Poppy at his heels. Over his shoulder, he called, "The name's Zeke. Zeke Soto."

Alexis exchanged glances with Keira, who raised her eyebrows in question. Alexis nodded, and without another word, they both followed the dog's example and trailed after Zeke.

What were a woman and a child doing wandering in the wilds of Alaska with no provisions? Zeke led the way to the cabin steps and stopped at the covered pot of creek water he'd prepared for drinking earlier by boiling it and letting it cool. And what did the woman mean by an incident? He couldn't help but notice the girl's swollen eyes and bandaged knee. Maybe she'd run away from their tour group at Leah Falls, and her mother chased after her to bring her back. If so, they had a terrible sense of direction.

There were quite a few cabins and a lodge on Pearson Lake, six miles upstream on the Pearson River. It was a popular put-in spot for rafters and kayakers who liked to run the white water farther

downriver just above Chapel Lake, either on their
own or with a tour. The Pearson Lake Lodge oper-
ated a water taxi that served the lake and the upper
few miles of the river, often dropping lodgers for
day trips to hike to Leah Falls or fish the river. But
the woman had mentioned a camp, so they must be
part of a float-trip group. No doubt the rest of their
group was out beating the bushes, looking for them.
Just what he needed—more company.

Zeke had come here for the specific purpose of
being alone, responsible for himself and no one else.
The only person he ever saw was the driver of the
water taxi who delivered a few groceries once a
month, and since Zeke met him riverside, even the
driver didn't know exactly where Zeke's place was
located. As far as Zeke was aware, his was the only
cabin between Pearson and Chapel Lakes. It was far
enough up the mountain that nobody camping along
the river had ever stumbled upon it. Until now.

"Wait here." He gathered two enamelware cups
and a bowl from inside his cabin. He used a dipper
to fill the first cup and offered it to the girl. When
she stepped up to take it, he noticed she was limping on the leg with the bandaged knee.

"Thank you." She gulped the water down greed-
ily. Now that he was closer, he could see that her eyes
weren't simply red from crying, but looked irritated
and swollen, likely from the bear spray in the car-
tridge she wore on her belt. Maybe a bear encounter
was the incident the woman had mentioned. But if

that were the case, why not just say so? But it was not his concern.

The second cup went to the woman, who also thanked him politely, and then he filled the bowl for the dog. At least they were savvy enough to know better than to drink untreated creek water, but the woman probably had no idea about the dangers they were getting into, wandering off from her guide or group. Maybe he should offer some advice. He re-filled the girl's cup and then held out his hand for the woman's water bottle. "Your party will be looking for you. When you're lost, it's better to stay in one place so they can find you."

"There's nobody else. It's just us," the girl said, and then she clapped her hand over her mouth and looked at the woman, who gave her a reassuring smile.

"It's okay, Keira." She handed her water bottle to Zeke. "She's right—no one is looking for us, but we're not lost. The trail that runs beside this creek is passable all the way to the river, yes?"

"That's right. Serendipity Creek runs into the Pearson River." He filled the bottle and handed it back.

She screwed on the lid and stowed it in her day pack. "Serendipity Creek. I like that. So, if we follow it to the river and then hike along the bank, we'll find our camp. No problem."

No problem, except that depending on where they'd camped, it could be several miles, and the girl, Keira, looked like she was coming to the end of her rope.

Zeke looked toward the mountain. They'd probably be fine. There were about three hours more of daylight, plenty of time for them to get back to camp, even moving slowly. If they didn't run into any more trouble. And if they could find their way. And was it his imagination, or were those clouds in the west beginning to look a little ominous?

The woman seemed confident of her ability to find the camp, but she had gotten them lost once already, and even though she was armed, he didn't like the thought of the two of them, alone, wandering along the riverbank at dusk, when the bears were most active. Once again, he tried to remind himself it was none of his concern, and yet he was concerned. Against his better judgment, he suggested, "Maybe you should stay here until morning."

"Here?" The woman's eyes went wide. "With you?"

"Just for the night. I'm not liking the looks of those clouds."

She turned to follow his gaze and frowned. "Yeah, I see what you mean. The forecast was for clear weather all week."

"Forecasts can change."

"That's true, especially in the mountains. But—"

"Look. I realize you don't know me, and I can see why you'd hesitate to stay, but I don't think you should have the girl out hiking near the river this late in the day when the salmon are running."

"And the grizzlies are roaming." The woman nodded, but she still looked undecided.

"I can give you the cabin and sleep outside if that would make you feel—" Her sudden laughter stopped him. It was a wonderful laugh, melodic, from deep in her chest, and it lit up her whole face, transforming it from conventionally pretty to extraordinary. Zeke found himself grinning. "What?"

"You. Ten minutes ago, you couldn't get rid of us fast enough. Now you're offering to sleep outside in the rain if it makes us more comfortable. What's that all about?"

A good question, one he was asking himself as well. "I guess I just don't want to feel responsible if anything bad happens to the two of you," he answered honestly.

"You aren't responsible." She put the emphasis on *you*, as though someone else was. There must be more to the incident she'd referred to earlier, but she clearly didn't want to talk about it. "And we'll be fine."

"Maybe so, but you must agree, the safest course is to stay until morning." He grinned. "Even if it does break the hermit code."

She looked chagrined. "You heard that?"

"I did. And she's right—I am a hermit, or at least a recluse. But I still think you should stay the night."

She looked again at the sky. "Those clouds are getting darker."

"If it helps with your decision—" he nodded toward the Dutch oven "—I'm serving hasenpfeffer and sourdough bread for dinner tonight." Good thing he'd gotten his monthly delivery of root vegetables last week, along with coffee, flour and other staples.

"What's hasenpfeffer?" Keira whispered to the woman.

"Rabbit stew," she told the girl. "It's delicious."

"I am hungry." Keira sniffed. "And it smells really good."

"Are you sure you have enough?" the woman asked Zeke.

"Sure. I'll just throw in another potato or two."

The woman laughed that extraordinary laugh again. "That's what my mother always used to say when we'd ask if friends could stay for dinner."

"Oh, yeah? Mine, too." Zeke hadn't thought about that in a long time.

Keira snorted. "Not mine. Mom's off potatoes. It's all rice cakes and kale. My friends know better than to eat at my house."

So the woman wasn't Keira's mother. Interesting. "So, shall I set three places at the table?"

The woman looked at the tiny cabin and around the clearing. "You have a table?"

Zeke chuckled. "I was speaking figuratively, but I do have enough bowls and spoons."

"Ah. In that case, we accept your generous invitation, and we very much appreciate the hospitality." She smiled at him. "I'm Alexis, this is Keira and the dog is Poppy. Thank you, Zeke."

Chapter Three

While the stew finished cooking, Zeke gathered up his tools and put them under a tarp to protect them from the possible rain. He used another tarp to cover a supply of firewood. Keira rested on a log near the fire with the dog at her feet, but Alexis prowled around the clearing. She'd already checked out the entire area.

She'd exclaimed over the little cave with a spring running through it that he used as a combination refrigerator and root cellar. But she'd also inspected the clothesline, the food cache in a tree, the woodpile and every trail into the forest. Even now, every so often, she would stop and listen and then, apparently satisfied, would continue patrolling the area around the cabins. Zeke got the feeling she was expecting trouble.

Should he ask? Her concerns weren't any of his business, but she was at his place now. Before he could make up his mind, she stopped to examine the notches where the logs fit together at the corners of his cabin-in-progress. It had taken him a lot of practice to learn to scribe the saddle notches properly, but he was pleased with the work he'd done. Alexis turned to him. "What is the gap for?"

"What's that?" After living alone all these months, Zeke wasn't used to conversation.

"The gaps between the logs. It's obvious you went to a great deal of trouble to craft the notch of each log to exactly fit the log below it, and so the gaps are no accident. Why didn't you want the log resting directly on the one below it?"

"Log cabins settle over time," he explained. "I'll fill the gaps with chinking, but over the next few years as they dry out, the logs will compress. Once they've finished settling, they'll fit together like a jigsaw puzzle. At least, that's the theory."

"Interesting." She ran a hand over the cut ends. "I'm not seeing any chainsaw marks."

"No."

She tilted her head to the right. "No power tools at all?"

Zeke shook his head. No power tools, no electricity, no running water. Just the same equipment a sourdough, an early prospector from over a hundred years ago, might have used to build a cabin. And many of the cabins they'd built were still standing.

He waited for the next question, the one asking why anyone would choose to live this way if he didn't have to, but it didn't come. Instead, she nodded toward the small cabin, where the logs weren't quite as well fitted. One corner sagged where the ground had washed out under it. "I see you had a bit of subsidence in that corner, but you must have corrected the problem on this one, because these logs seem perfectly level."

Interesting that she would notice that. "I took some shortcuts on the first cabin, just to get a shelter up quickly, and I didn't prepare the ground as carefully as I should have. I plan to shore it up there and use it as a storage shed once I get the main one built."

"Makes sense. Will the main cabin have a sod roof as well?"

"That's the plan. It's surprisingly waterproof. Why all the questions?"

She gave a dazzling smile. "Just professional interest, I guess."

"You're a professional log cabin builder?"

"No, a structural engineer. I've never really gotten an up close look at a traditional log cabin. It's fascinating." She traced along the belly of the log where he'd planed it to fit with the log below. "You're a real craftsman."

It was nice to have someone appreciate the care he'd put into his work. For a moment Zeke felt a glow of pride, until he remembered where pride had led him once before. He turned and walked to the Dutch oven. "I'll see if the stew is ready. If you'd like to grab some bowls and spoons, they're in the cabin."

"All right." She crossed the clearing to the small

cabin, but looked over her shoulder at him once, as though she wasn't quite sure what to make of him. He could sympathize—he wasn't sure what to make of her, either. She seemed competent, levelheaded. She was an engineer, and the engineers he'd known tended to be careful planners. And yet here she was, lost in the woods without proper equipment, and with a child, no less. It didn't make sense.

The stew was done. Zeke gave it a stir and ladled it into the blue enamelware bowls Alexis had brought outside. "Thank you. This smells amazing," Alexis said as she took two of the bowls, handed one to Keira and sat down beside her. Zeke sat down on a nearby log and dipped his spoon into his bowl.

"Would you mind if I said grace?" Alexis asked Zeke.

Zeke put his spoon down, embarrassed, although he wasn't sure why he should be. "Sure. Go ahead."

Alexis reached for Keira's hand and closed her eyes. "Dear Lord, we thank You for today, for showing us the way to safety and for guiding us here. Thank You for bringing us to Zeke, for his generosity and for this wonderful food he's sharing. Please bless us and keep us. In Your name we pray. Amen."

"Amen," Keira and Zeke echoed simultaneously. He had gotten out of the habit of saying grace, figuring God already knew what was in his mind, but there was something concrete in saying the words aloud. It was a reminder that even though he'd come to this place to get closer to God, he still felt the same distance between them. It was a barrier he couldn't seem to cross.

Keira took her first bite. "This is really good."

Zeke's first taste confirmed that the stew was acceptable, but nothing noteworthy. His spice collection consisted of salt and pepper. But what was that saying, something about hunger being the best sauce? Judging by the speed at which they were eating, both of his guests had worked up quite an appetite.

The dog was lying at their feet, but her ears were pricked. After glancing to make sure Alexis was busy eating, Keira dropped a chunk of rabbit meat and the dog caught it in the air. He smiled to himself. He had some salmon he had smoked and dried that had turned out more like leather than salmon jerky, but it would make good dog food. After dinner, he'd make sure the Labrador had a full stomach, too.

Once Alexis had eaten several bites, she set her spoon down, and with studied casualness she asked, "So, Zeke. Tell me about your neighbors."

"What neighbors?"

"Is there anyone else who lives in this area?"

"No. The closest would be the people up at Pearson Lake."

"Nobody who lives over by Leah Falls?" she probed.

"No, although Leah Falls does draw hikers, either rafters or day-trippers from the lake."

"Day-trippers here?"

"Yes. The river is still deep enough for powerboats up to this point. The lodge sometimes brings guests to hike and fish. I have an arrangement with the guy who runs the store there to bring me groceries once a month."

"I see. Do you know many of the people up at Pearson Lake? Are any of them dangerous?"

Dangerous? "Why? What happened?"

Alexis paused as though to weigh her words, but Keira broke in. "A man grabbed me and tried to drag me into the woods, and Alexis saw another guy waiting there. I sprayed him with bear spray, and we ran."

That explained a lot. "I'm sorry to hear that. Did they hurt you?"

"No." Keira looked at her knee. "This was when I fell later."

"I'm sorry," he repeated. "To answer your question, I only know a few people from the lake, and I can't imagine any of them attacking someone. Did you fly in there?"

"Yes."

"Then you know it's a popular floatplane landing, and there's a lodge, so people are always coming and going. What did the men look like?"

Keira looked at Alexis, who shrugged. "I was up at the top of the pass and Keira was in the meadow just above the tree line when it happened. I never got close enough to see features, and I think his face was covered."

Keira nodded. "He was wearing a buff, and he had on a cap and sunglasses. Jeans and a black T-shirt."

"Good description. You're observant," Zeke noted. "What about the other man?"

"All I could really distinguish were his orange hiking boots," Alexis said.

"Did they chase you?"

"For a bit, I think. Once we made it to a game trail in the woods, I couldn't see them anymore. I thought I heard shouts, but I'm not sure how far they followed after us." Alexis let out a breath. "Honestly, I was afraid to stop and find out."

"Understandable." Now it all made sense. How they'd found themselves lost in the woods without enough water or food. Why they'd wandered over to the creek that ran beside his property. No wonder they'd looked frightened when they realized he'd seen them lurking behind the cabin. "I'm wondering. Do you think this attacker was lying in wait, or just happened upon a girl alone in the meadow?" He tried to keep his voice matter-of-fact, although inside he was shuddering, thinking of what they might have done to the girl if she hadn't gotten away.

Alexis tipped her head to the right and seemed to think before answering. "Good question. We haven't seen any other campers on the river, and we didn't tell anyone we were hiking, so they couldn't really have been waiting."

"The guy, the one in the meadow, came up the trail behind us," Keira said. "When he saw me, he waved and said something about it being a nice day. Poppy kind of growled, but I thought it was because he had that buff over his face, like some people use to keep the dust out of their mouths, although it wasn't dusty on the trail. He started to walk on by, and then all of a sudden, he ran over and grabbed my arm."

"Did he say anything else?" Zeke asked.

Keira shrugged. "'Come with me,' or something like that."

"If they came up the trail, it must have been a crime of opportunity," Alexis stated. "And if they were day-trippers, like Zeke says, they've probably already returned to the lodge. How much farther can the powerboats go downstream?" she asked him.

"The confluence of Serendipity Creek is the limit. There's a sandbar, and then the river gets rocky soon after that."

"Okay, so most likely, they've given up." Her features relaxed a bit. "But just in case, tomorrow we'll take the raft downriver past the first rapids where they can't get to us. Sound like a plan?" she asked Keira.

The girl nodded, clearly relieved to think the danger had passed. "And you've got your gun if they come back."

Alexis touched the revolver in her holster. "I do."

"Okay." Keira ran her hand over the dog's head. "But I'm glad we're staying here tonight instead of in the tent at the river."

Alexis smiled at Zeke. "So am I."

Zeke was right; a sod roof was surprisingly waterproof. As Alexis lay still, listening to the raindrops drum against the chimney pipe, she wondered what sort of underlayment he'd used between the rough boards that formed the ceiling of the little cabin and the sod over the top. Probably not a modern roofing membrane, since everything else about these cabins used techniques from the turn of the last century. Most likely tar paper, which, as she recalled from one of her college textbooks, was first used during the California gold rush in the 1800s. Whatever it was, it seemed to be working.

The walls, maybe not quite as well. Zeke had chinked between the logs, but in the one sagging corner, some of the chinking had fallen out, and occasional gusts blew rain through the gaps. Fortunately, it was the opposite corner from where they were sleeping. The woodstove at the foot of the bed, the type designed for wall tents, kept it cozy. In Alaska, rainfall was usually gentle, but occasionally a storm like this happened, with a sudden downpour and swirling winds. Alexis said a silent prayer of thanks that she and Keira were here, in this sturdy little cabin, instead of in their tent on the riverbank. She just hoped the tent stakes held, or else the tent would be history and the two of them would be sleeping under a tarp for the rest of the trip. Granted, that would only be for one more night.

Even though she and Zeke agreed that the danger was probably past, she wasn't taking any more risks with Keira. They'd planned to take a week on a leisurely float with days off for fishing and hiking.

Instead, they would spend tomorrow getting as far down the Pearson River as possible, spend the night above the biggest rapids, and then shoot the canyon the next morning and make their way to Chapel Lake. As soon as she could get her hands on her satellite phone, she'd call the floatplane company to arrange for an early pickup there.

This trip was turning out to be a far cry from what Alexis had expected. She'd hoped this would be a week of bonding with Keira. Keira was at that confusing age, starting the transition from girl to woman. Alexis had wanted to take the time away from cell phones and daily life to talk and listen to Keira's hopes and concerns, to teach Keira skills and build her confidence in herself, and to show her how strong she could be. The two strangers in the woods had stolen that opportunity.

Or had they? When the man grabbed Keira, she hadn't given up. Instead, she'd used her bear spray to get away. And she'd run for miles, even though she'd already been tired from the climb. Keira had risen to the challenge, and while Alexis would have never wished it to happen, now that it was behind them, maybe there was a lesson here. Proof that Keira was strong and resourceful, able to handle whatever life threw her way. Alexis would try to help her niece see it that way.

The rain stopped, and in the sudden silence Alexis could hear Keira's even breathing as she slept beside her on the narrow bunk. Poor kid was exhausted. They hadn't let Zeke sleep out in the rain, but he had insisted that they take the bunk while he and Poppy slept on a mat on the dirt floor of the cabin. A gentleman. But who was he, really? Alaska had its fair share of loners—people, usually men, who for one reason or another chose to isolate themselves far from others. More than a few were running from something. She wondered if this was true of Zeke, although he seemed kind and gentle. One of the five books on a shelf near the bed was a well-worn Bible, which she took as a good sign. So why was he here?

It was funny. After today, sleeping in the same room as a strange man should have been nerve-racking, but it wasn't. She felt safe in this tiny cabin with Zeke, confident that God had brought them to this place of sanctuary.

A sudden snort was followed by a whimper as Poppy twitched, probably chasing rabbits in her dreams. A quiet chuckle followed. "Zeke?" she whispered. "Are you awake?"

"Yes," he whispered back.

"Sorry for kicking you out of your bed."

"It's okay. That's not why I'm awake."

"Why, then?"

"Just thinking. I don't sleep a lot."

"What are you thinking about?" A personal question, but somehow not being able to see him emboldened her enough to ask.

He took a beat before answering. "Life. Death. God."

"Wow, big thoughts. No wonder you can't sleep."

"Yeah." He chuckled again. "You should get some rest, though. You have a big day tomorrow."

Tomorrow. She and Keira would find their way to the campsite and move downriver. Once they were past the smaller rapids, they were safe from anyone in a powerboat. Yes, tomorrow would be a big day. "That's true. Thank you for feeding us and letting us stay here tonight."

"My pleasure. Good night, Alexis."

"Good night, Zeke." She turned on her side. Almost immediately, she was asleep.

Alexis woke the next morning to birdsong and a ray of sunshine slipping through the narrow opening under the eaves. Keira still slept beside her, but Zeke and Poppy were no longer on the mat beside the bed. Alexis slipped out from under the blanket as carefully as she could. Keira moaned and turned on her side, but immediately dropped off again. Good. She needed all the rest she could get.

Outside, a campfire was burning. Zeke must have had the foresight to shelter some firewood from last night's rain. A few drops still clung to the waxy leaves of a balsam poplar at the edge of the clearing, catching the morning sun and reflecting like diamonds. The air had that fresh-washed scent, like the earth was brand-new, created just that morning especially for them.

Zeke appeared, carrying a large bucket of water, with Poppy at his heels. After he'd fed the dog dried salmon last night, Zeke was her new favorite person. "Good morning. How is Keira?"

"Still sleeping." Alexis stooped to pet the dog.

"Probably for the best." He set the bucket down. After arranging a grate over the fire, he set a large pot on top and poured in the water from the bucket. "And how about you?"

"Me? I'm fine." She straightened.

"I'm glad. I know something like what happened yesterday can be traumatic."

She shrugged. "It's over now."

He nodded and poured more water from the bucket into a tall pot with a spout, which he also set on the grate to heat. "It will take a while for the water to boil, but then we'll have coffee."

"That sounds wonderful." She smiled. "Since you're doing everything authentic to 1900 or so, I wasn't sure if coffee was on the menu."

"Sourdoughs did, in fact, bring coffee or tea, but I confess, I'm not a purist when it comes to food. In my monthly grocery delivery, I get carrots, onions, potatoes and dried fruit along with my pilot biscuits and dried beans." He didn't quite smile, but his eyes crinkled in the corners. "I'm not inclined to risk scurvy in the name of authenticity."

"Wise move. I'm sure they would have done the same if they had the choice." Alexis rearranged the items in her day pack to distribute the weight more evenly. "Once Keira's up, we'll head out. I can't thank you enough for letting us stay the night."

"You've already thanked me. And there's no reason to run off hungry. Once the water's boiled, I plan to make sourdough pancakes with birch syrup."

"Wow! Homemade pancakes? I'll have to post five stars for accommodations."

"Yeah, I get that a lot." His delivery was so deadpan, Alexis almost missed the joke. When she laughed, he looked pleased. He didn't comment further as he poked the fire and added more wood. Alexis stretched and walked around the area, working out the kinks, before she settled on the log. It felt oddly companionable, hanging out by the fire, waiting for coffee. Poppy came to sit beside Alexis, but she kept an eye on Zeke. She wouldn't want to miss another treat.

Zeke had just added coffee grounds to the pot and returned it to the fire when Keira stepped outside, rubbing her eyes. As she put weight on her bad knee, she winced. Not good, but Alexis tried to project a positive attitude. "Hi, sleepyhead. Little bit stiff today?" She went to help Keira down the steps.

"Yeah. My knee hurts." Holding Alexis's hand, Keira hopped down the steps on her good leg and limped over to sit on the log.

"Let's see." Alexis removed the bandage, and the dog thrust her head closer to take a sniff. Alexis pushed her out of the way. "I appreciate your interest, Poppy, but it's hard to see past you. Okay, the scrape looks good. No infection. But the knee might be a little swollen." She gave Keira a smile. "Let's see how you feel after breakfast. Zeke says he's making pancakes."

"Pancakes?" Keira perked up. "I love pancakes."

"Then I'd better get busy." Zeke first poured a cup of coffee and handed it to Alexis, then removed a dipper of water from the big pot, which was now boiling, and carried it to a bowl he'd left sitting on a stump. Once he'd stirred the water into whatever was in the bowl, he returned to move the pot off the grate and replaced it with a griddle. Twenty minutes later, Keira offered a short grace, and they all sat down to stacks of pancakes.

"This birch syrup is excellent," Alexis told him. "Did you make it?"

He nodded. "My first experiment. I tapped the trees right after I arrived in April. It turned out a lot better than the salmon jerky."

"Poppy would disagree. She's in love with that salmon."

He gave the dog a pat. "She's a forgiving food critic."

After breakfast, Alexis and Keira prepared to go, filling Alexis's water bottle with boiled water and packing some of Zeke's salmon jerky for Poppy. Keira pulled on her day pack, but she was still favoring one leg. It was going to be a long, slow hike. At Zeke's suggestion, she chose a sturdy branch to use as a walking staff. While she made use of the outhouse one last time, Zeke approached Alexis.

"How far upriver is your camp?" he asked.

"It's near the base of the Leah Falls Trail. About three miles, you said?"

"Maybe two and a half at the river, but you've got at least that far from here to reach the river." He pressed his lips together and seemed to be having an internal argument. Finally, he spoke. "If you want, you can leave Keira with me. You can go on ahead and bring your boat to the mouth of Serendipity Creek, so she doesn't have to cover the miles along the river. Meanwhile, I can hike down with her to meet you at the creek."

Alexis considered. That would save a lot of wear and tear on Keira's already painful knee, but could she leave Keira with a strange man? Granted, after sharing his cabin and feeding them pancakes, Zeke seemed more like a friend than a stranger, but what did she really know about him? But as she watched Keira limp her way across the clearing, she saw the wisdom of the plan.

When she didn't answer immediately, he added, "I'd go and let you stay with her, except I don't know much about boats."

"No, that makes sense. Keira, Zeke has offered to hike with you down to the river while I go break down camp and bring the raft closer to save you some steps. Are you all right with that?"

"Okay," Keira answered immediately. "Do you have a gun like Alexis's in case of bears?"

"I do," he assured her, and Alexis knew they weren't only talking about bears. "But the bears tend to stay near the river where the salmon are. There's no run up Serendipity Creek, so they don't wander up here too often."

Keira touched her holster. "I've got my bear spray, just in case."

"Good. I'm hopeful neither of us will need to use them."

"So, probably an hour and a half to reach camp," Alexis said, calculating the time. "Two hours to break down camp and pack the boat, and another half hour to float to the mouth of the creek. I'll meet you there in four hours, roughly?"

"Sounds good," Zeke answered. "We'll hang around here for a while and then head down. Be careful."

"Same to you. Keira, we'll go through some class two white water this afternoon."

Keira grinned. "Can't wait."

"Good. See you both soon. Thank you, Zeke."

"Anytime."

Poppy followed her down the trail for a few steps, but then she paused and whined, looking back. Alexis said, "Good idea, Poppy. You stay with Keira."

The dog immediately turned around and trotted back to camp. Whether it was because of her loyalty to Keira or hopes for more salmon, it was hard to say, but Alexis felt better knowing both Zeke and Poppy were looking out for Keira. Keeping her safe.

Chapter Four

Zeke and Keira watched until Alexis rounded a boulder and disappeared into the woods. Then he turned to the girl. Now what? He'd offered to let her stay because she was limping, but he had little experience with girls that age. Or any age, really. He'd noticed Alexis's hesitation before agreeing to let Keira stay, but she'd decided to trust him, and he wanted to live up to that trust. He tried a smile. "Okay, then. Shouldn't take us more than an hour to get to the river. You want some more pancakes?"

"No, thanks. They were good, though. I can, like, wash dishes or something while you work," Keira suggested.

"Okay. Let me get you set up." That was easy. He got out the equipment and left her to it while he went to work peeling the bark from the tree he'd downed the day before.

Before long, she'd finished the dishes and wandered over to watch him. "What's that thing you're using?"

"It's called a drawknife. See, this part in the middle is sharp, so it cuts through the bark, and it has handles on both ends so you can draw it toward yourself to use it."

"Can I try?"

"Um…" She was a kid, and the blade was razor-sharp. "Better not. But if you want to tidy up the bark so I can move it to my kindling pile, it would really help." And shouldn't put too much stress on her knee.

"Okay." She gathered the shreds into a pile and then stopped to watch him. "My dad has a bunch of tools, but his all run on batteries or motors."

"Power tools are useful, but I like hand tools. They're quieter, for one thing, so I can still hear the birds and creek sounds while I work."

She shrugged. "Daddy never uses his tools, anyway."

"No?"

"He's too busy. He's Dixon Mahoney, head of Mahoney Tours."

"Is he?" Mahoney Tours, huh. Zeke knew of them, of course. It seemed like you could hardly move around Alaska anymore without seeing a Mahoney Tours lodge or bus or boat trailer. Zeke could remember when they were just a niche adventure tour company, but in the last decade or so, they'd mushroomed into the dominant tourist business in the state. "I'll bet that does keep him busy."

"Yeah. I'm supposed to be with him this week and next, but he had to go to Juneau, so Alexis said she'd take me on this raft trip instead. Alexis used to work as a river guide, but she's an engineer now."

Former river guide. That explained Alexis's confident manner in the outdoors. "What relation is Alexis to you?"

"She's my aunt. We do lots of stuff together. She took my friends Elise and Sarah and me to a concert last month." She huffed. "Daddy was supposed to take me to the concert at the square in Anchorage tonight, but that was before he went on his trip and Alexis took me rafting. He got me a new phone, though, to make up for it. They just released this model last week. None of my friends have it yet. Want to see?"

"Sure." Zeke had no interest in cell phones, but he stopped stripping bark long enough to pretend to admire it, since it seemed important to her.

"I got the gold one, and this case is, like, super-tough and waterproof. The battery's dead on the phone, so I can't show you what it can do, but isn't it cool?" She stroked the phone like it was a pet.

"Very cool," Zeke agreed, although he was more impressed with the case than the phone. Pretty expensive gadget for a kid. At what age did kids get cell phones these days, anyway? "What grade are you in?"

"I'm going into sixth this fall." A little line formed

between her eyebrows. "That's middle school. It's kinda scary."

"Why is that?" he asked, curious as to what a girl who had run off a potential attacker with bear spray would find scary.

She shrugged. "I don't know. I've only ever been in one school before. This will be different."

"Sure, but the kids you'll be in class with will be facing the same thing. They're probably just as scared." He grinned. "Besides, you're tough."

"You think so?"

"Oh, yeah. A regular *tejónita*."

"*Tejónita?* What's that?"

"It's a nickname my grandfather used to call my mother sometimes. It means 'little badger.'"

"And badgers are tough?"

"Definitely. Once I saw a badger stare down a bear. I think the bear knew he'd win in a fight, but when the badger didn't back down, the bear decided it wasn't worth the trouble and wandered off."

"*Tejónita.* I like that." Keira smiled to herself as she returned her treasured phone to her pocket. "What kind of phone do you have?"

He chuckled. "I don't have a phone."

"No way. Really?"

Funny that she'd taken cooking over a fire and not using power tools in stride, but she couldn't imagine life without a phone. "What good would a cell phone do me way out here? There are no cell towers," he pointed out.

"Alexis has a satellite phone on the raft, and it works anywhere. Don't you have one of those?"

"No."

"Why not?"

"Sat phones run on batteries, and batteries need electricity to charge. Besides, I don't have anyone I need to talk to."

"Nobody? Don't you have a family?"

"No." At least, no family he was in touch with. A few aunts, uncles and cousins, but he'd left them behind when he moved to Alaska.

"Friends?"

"Not really."

"You don't talk to anybody at all? Like, Alexis and me are the first people you've talked to since you got here?"

"There's a guy who brings my groceries up the river once a month."

"What's his name?"

"Uh…" What was his name? "Chuck."

"And you talk to Chuck?"

"Sure." They always exchanged a few words, along with money and next month's list. That counted, right?

"So, you only talk to one guy, and you hardly remember his name."

Zeke shrugged.

Keira studied him like he was some sort of exotic animal. "How long have you been here, anyway?"

"Since April."

"It's August now." She counted on her fingers. "May, June, July... Like, four months?"

"Sounds about right." He shaved another strip from the log.

"How long are you staying here?"

Ah, that was the big question, wasn't it? Was this just an interlude, a temporary penance while he tried to get right with God once again, or was this his life now? Was it even possible to get right with God after what he'd done? He'd come here for a simpler life, a way to close the chasm he felt between himself and God, but sometimes that chasm seemed wider than ever.

Chuck had informed him that the September 1 delivery would be his last for the season. So, at that time, Zeke could either catch a ride back to Pearson Lake with him or hunker down for a winter alone.

And while it might get lonely here at the cabin, at least here Zeke couldn't hurt anyone, because he wasn't responsible for anyone else. Until now, anyway. But in a few hours, he would deliver Keira back to her aunt, they would be on their way and he would be alone again. Just how he wanted it. "Right now I'm concentrating on getting the main cabin built. And then we'll see."

"You're weird." Keira laughed. "But Alexis says everybody's weird and that's what makes life so interesting."

"Is that so?"

"Uh-huh, because weird just means different, and

she says God made everybody different and He loves us all." She tilted her head, mirroring the gesture he'd noticed several times from her aunt. "But she usually says that to make me feel better when I'm upset about something."

"Does it work?"

"Sometimes." She smirked. "And sometimes I get mad at her for trying to cheer me up. But even then, I usually end up laughing."

"It sounds like you have a pretty special aunt."

"Yeah, she's weird, too, in a good way."

"Weird in a good way." Zeke chuckled. "I like that."

"You're weird in a good way, too," Keira said decidedly.

"Oh?"

"Absolutely. You're like a time traveler who doesn't know about modern technology, but you're really good at all this old-fashioned stuff. And you helped us when we needed help. You're a good friend."

"Thank you, Tejónita." Zeke smiled at her. "I'm honored to be your friend."

Alexis made good time on the way down to the river. The game trail she and Keira had been following along the creek grew wider after Zeke's cabin, probably from Zeke's steps to and from the river to fish and collect his groceries. At the confluence of the creek and Pearson River, someone—presumably

Zeke—had built a floating dock from logs to make it easier for a boat to land. Just downstream, a sandbar inches below the surface effectively cut off any further access for powerboats. She would probably need to partially unload the raft to portage it over the sandbar. Maybe Zeke would help push.

From there, Alexis simply followed the riverbank upstream until she reached camp. That trail was rougher, especially since last night's rain had swollen the river and covered parts of the trail, forcing her to detour around and through the brush. Good thing she'd tied the raft to a sturdy tree before leaving camp. The wind and rain last night might have swept it downriver if she hadn't.

She stopped once to eat the energy bar from her backpack, glad she'd saved it yesterday. At one point she was forced to scramble over a scree pile. None of this would have been easy for Keira to manage with an injured knee, so it was good they'd taken Zeke up on his offer. After what had happened, Alexis hated to let Keira out of her sight, but she felt confident that her niece would be safe with Zeke. She wasn't sure exactly why. Was it the kindness she saw in his brown eyes? The gentle way he stroked Poppy's head? Or was it something more fundamental, some assurance that God had put them on a path to find Zeke because he could help them? Whatever it was, she trusted him.

What was his story? It was all so unexpected. What was he doing alone in the woods? Why was he building his cabin with no power tools and no technology? Was it simply a personal challenge to see if it could be done? Somehow, she sensed some deeper reason than that. He masked it well, but occasionally his expression would reveal a fundamental sadness, an internal burden of some sort. She prayed that God would help him heal from whatever had caused that pain.

She arrived at the campsite and was glad to see the tent had survived the storm with only a minor tear in the rain flap. The sleeping bags inside were a little damp in places, but they'd dry. The camp stove, folding chairs, water filter and other equipment seemed fine. The bears didn't appear to have bothered the food they'd left cached between trees, so they were good there. She made her way past some bushes to the shoreline where they'd left the boat, and stopped in shock.

The raft had been ripped to shreds!

Alexis just stood there for a moment, taking in the damage. A bear must have come along and mistaken their only means of transportation for a blow-up toy. The inflatable floor was still intact, but all three air chambers that formed the body of the raft had been sliced apart, the tough fabric hanging in strips from the oar frame. Even the thwarts that crossed the center of the boat had been punctured. The bowline was still secured to a tree, but the other end was knotted through a D ring that now hung limp from the collapsed tube.

Slowly, she turned her eyes to the rest of the scene. The oars had been dragged away from the boat, but they didn't seem to be bent or cracked. A red dry bag lay on the bank, the comprehensive first aid kit that had been inside half spilling out the opening. Extra clothes, hats and sunglasses were scattered around the area, whether by the bear or last night's wind, it was hard to say.

She spotted something blue half hidden in a nearby bush. It turned out to be the sack that contained her patch kit. For a moment, hope flickered. As always when she prepared for a raft trip, Alexis had purchased a new jar of glue since the adhesive tended to dry up over the winter. But the store had been out of the half-pint-sized cans she usually bought, and she'd had to buy a whole quart. Maybe God had been looking out for them. But the flame of hope died when she remembered she'd only included the usual number of patches, enough to repair a gouge or two from a sharp rock or a puncture from a broken tree branch but not to rebuild an entire raft.

Almost on autopilot, she began gathering the scattered gear. Embedded in a bush, she found a green dry bag still rolled and snapped closed. Inside, a week's worth of emergency freeze-dried meals were still sealed and ready for use. Good news because it looked like they might be here for a while. She was grateful the bear hadn't torn into that bag...which, now that she thought about it, seemed odd.

Sure, between the hermetically sealed packaging

of the meals and the heavy dry bag she'd stored them in, the food wouldn't have emitted a strong odor, but bears had a keen sense of smell. Alexis had left the dry bag in the raft, feeling confident that a bear casually passing wouldn't detect the food inside, but it seemed strange that a bear had torn the raft apart and then thrown this bag of food, undamaged, into the brush.

She set that bag aside and went to check the red dry bag, the one she'd packed with a first aid kit, binoculars, a camera with a telephoto lens for photographing wildlife, extra batteries, the solar charger and a satellite phone. The phone! She'd almost forgotten about the phone!

The bag was open, the buckle unsnapped and the top unrolled. The first aid kit at the top seemed undamaged. Alexis frowned. Bears were clever animals, but no bear would know how to unlatch a buckle. She tried to think back to the last time she or Keira would have used the bag. Probably when she took out the camera with the telephoto lens to photograph some eagles sitting together in a tree on their first day. But she was sure after she'd returned the camera to the bag, she would have rolled the top and buckled it. She wouldn't have risked ruining her favorite camera with water spray.

Carefully she emptied the bag. The camera was there, but the lens cover had fallen off. Batteries, charger, binoculars. No phone. Surely she was mistaken. She shook the bag and then reached in to feel around, but it was empty.

Alexis sat back on her heels, thinking. There was no way she forgot to pack the phone. The phone, throw rope and first aid kit were essential safety equipment, right at the top of her packing list. And no bear had unbuckled that bag to steal the phone. She went to examine the raft more closely. The tubes had been torn to shreds all right, but not in even lines like a set of claws would do. Instead, it looked like a knife had deliberately slashed the tubes in several places. No bear had done this. It was done by human vandals.

With her hand on her revolver, she made a sweep around the camp, looking for more evidence, but any footprints, bear or human, must have washed away in the rain last night. She'd seen no sign of anyone along the riverfront she'd traversed that morning. The same two men who had accosted Keira had to have torn up the camp. Anything else would be too big of a coincidence.

She returned the camera, binoculars and other items to the dry bag, sealed it up and left it. If the vandals hadn't taken off with the stuff before, they probably weren't coming back for it. Then she gathered what she could make the most use of—the UV water purifier, food, dog kibble, solar charger, a few clothes, and toothbrushes—and crammed them all into one of the sleeping bag's stuff sacks so she could sling it over her shoulder. At the last minute, she threw in a box of Alaska trivia cards she'd brought along, too, since it looked like they might have some time to kill.

She had to get back to Keira and Zeke. Together, they'd figure out what to do next.

Chapter Five

Zeke checked the position of the sun. He'd gotten the bark stripped from the log, fed Keira a lunch of leftover stew and pancakes, and listened to a long dissertation on the relative merits of various social media stars. At least, he thought that was who they were; he didn't recognize any of the names. But Keira remained undaunted by his utter lack of knowledge. In fact, she seemed to take it as a personal challenge to educate him on which names had been trending recently. Despite having no idea what she was talking about, he'd rather enjoyed listening to her cheerful chirping while he worked.

But now it was time to head out to meet Alexis at the mouth of the creek. He put away his tools and loaded his rifle, just in case. "Keira, time to go."

"Already? That went fast." Keira tightened her shoelaces and shrugged into her day pack. "Come on, Poppy."

The dog got up from where she'd been napping in the shade of the cabin and stretched, her head low over her front paws and tail high in the air. Zeke watched Keira cross the clearing toward him. She still limped a little, but she was moving better than she had been first thing this morning. The scrape on her knee looked like it was healing fine. "Got your walking staff?"

"Oh, I forgot." She trotted over to retrieve the staff, which confirmed to him that the knee couldn't be bothering her too much, and they started down the trail.

They'd only gone a mile or so when he heard movement up ahead. He signaled for Keira to be still. She grabbed Poppy's collar and nodded. Zeke crept forward, easing around the edge of some alders to see who or what was up ahead. "Alexis." He relaxed. "I thought we were meeting at the river."

She was carrying a bag slung over her shoulder, and her smile looked grim. "That was the plan. Now we need to make a new one."

"What happened?" Keira had followed him despite his signal to stay back. Poppy ran forward to greet Alexis.

She bent down to fondle the dog's ears. "There's a problem with the raft." She looked up and met Zeke's eyes. "I don't suppose you happen to have a satellite phone."

"He doesn't," Keira answered for him. "He doesn't even have a cell phone, if you can believe it." Keira chuckled, still amused at his lack of technology. Obviously, she hadn't yet realized the repercussions of this newest development.

"Your raft is damaged?" Zeke asked Alexis.

"Not just damaged. Destroyed. Someone sliced it to pieces."

"A bear?" he asked.

Alexis glanced at Keira and gave a little head shake. So not a bear. "I have a good patch kit," she answered indirectly, "but not nearly enough patches."

"I see." He needed more information, but he understood why she didn't want to have this discussion in front of her niece. The poor kid had already been scared enough. "Let's head back, then. I'll bet you could use a cup of coffee. I know I could. Here, let me carry that."

"Coffee sounds great." Alexis shot a grateful smile in his direction and passed him the bag.

They returned to the cabins. Zeke built up the fire. Alexis put a hand on Keira's face and tilted up her chin. "Your eyes look a whole lot better than they did yesterday. How do they feel?"

"Fine. My knee is better, too."

"Good."

"Say, Keira?" Zeke picked up his speckled coffeepot. "Would you mind fetching us some water from the creek for coffee?"

"Okay." Keira took the pot and trotted toward the creek with Poppy keeping her company.

Once she was out of earshot, Zeke asked, "What happened to the raft?"

"Someone sliced up the tubes. I thought it was a bear at first, but then I realized my satellite phone is missing."

"And you don't think a bear could have carried it away?" Unlikely, but not impossible.

"Not unless he unbuckled the dry bag and re-packed the other items after removing the phone."

Zeke shook his head. "Bears can be pretty inge-nious, but I've never known one that picked up after himself. And you're sure you packed the sat phone?"

"Positive."

"Okay." He'd take her word on that. Which meant that some human had maliciously destroyed their only means of transportation. The one sign of any other humans in the area lately had been the two men who attacked Keira. He didn't like this. Not at all. "You realize—"

"That the guys from Leah Falls probably did this?"

"Exactly."

"I know. But I didn't see any sign of them. They probably got their revenge by slicing up the raft and then hightailed it back to Pearson Lake. Hopefully, they've flown out by now."

"Hopefully. But that still leaves you stranded. You can get a ride out with the guy who brings me gro-ceries. Unfortunately, my regular delivery date is on the first of the month, which means he won't be back for another three weeks."

"We'll be out before that," Alexis assured him. "When we don't meet the floatplane at Chapel Lake in four days, they'll start looking for us."

"That's good." Of course, that assumed the weather held. August was notoriously rainy, and while a little rain wouldn't stop the search, planes and helicopters couldn't fly with low cloud ceilings. Sometimes respect for the weather could be the difference between life and death, as Zeke knew only too well. If he'd only— But he wouldn't think about that right now. Alexis needed reassurance, not doom and gloom. "With Mahoney Tours' resources behind you—"

Alexis frowned. "How do you know about Mahoney Tours?"

"Keira told me her dad was Dixon Mahoney. Why? Is it a secret?"

"Not exactly." Alexis shifted her weight to her other foot. "It's just that I don't usually tell people I'm one of 'those' Mahoneys. I don't actually own any part of the company anymore, but people hear the name and assume I have money and connections. Which I guess I do, in this case, because when my brother gets the report that we're missing, he'll get a search going right away."

"Is your brother your only emergency contact?"

"Him and Keira's mother, Mara. They're divorced."

"So, no boyfriend or husband waiting at home?"

The question slipped out before Zeke could remind himself it was none of his business.

"No boyfriends or husbands." Alexis gave a little smirk. "How about you? A vengeful ex-wife or two you're hiding from in the wilds of Alaska?"

"Nope. No wives. Not a living soul, in fact, who knows or cares exactly where I am right now." He had a few family members out there, but they'd lost touch years ago. After the accident, he'd driven off all his friends. Well, that wasn't quite true. Roger, who lived at Chapel Lake, knew where he was and hadn't quite given up on him yet, but Roger would respect his privacy. Realizing Alexis was looking at him with concern, Zeke cracked a smile. "It's part of the hermit code, you know."

"I see. Well, speaking of the hermit code..." Alexis paused. "It looks like we're grounded for a few days. If you want Keira and me to go—"

"I don't." He was sure of that. She was probably right that the attackers were gone, but he still didn't want her and Keira alone in a tent. And that was assuming their tent was still intact. She'd only mentioned the raft, but the vandals could have done more damage.

"Are you sure?" She searched his face. "I get the distinct impression you weren't thrilled the first time you laid eyes on us."

He chuckled. "Hmm, well, the two of you have grown on me."

"Have we?"

"Sure. I'll consider it an educational interlude. Another day or two of Keira's company, and I'll be up-to-date with all the hottest bands and internet stars."

She laughed. "Keep in mind, Keira is twelve. Her taste in music may be a little questionable."

"You're talking about questionable taste?" Keira had returned. She set the coffeepot over the fire and turned a mock glare toward Alexis, hands on her hips. "What was the last movie you saw—" Alexis started to answer, but Keira held up a finger "—that you didn't go to with me?"

"Um…oh, that one about ancient architecture."

"That doesn't count. It was a documentary. What real movie have you seen?"

"Documentaries are real movies," Alexis replied with a smile that suggested this wasn't the first time they'd had this discussion.

Keira turned her palms up and caught Zeke's eye. "You see? She's a total nerd."

"I do see." Zeke laughed. "But that's what makes life interesting, right?"

"Exactly!" Alexis held up a hand, and after a moment's hesitation, Zeke slapped her a high five.

Keira shook her head as though they were both hopeless. She sat down on the log and ran a hand over Poppy's head. "Okay, so you've had an opportunity to talk. How are we getting out of here without the raft?"

Zeke should have realized they couldn't keep the

truth from Keira. Judging from Alexis's sheepish smile, she was thinking the same. "When we don't show for the pickup, your dad will send out a search party. In the meantime, Zeke says we can stay here."

"Do you think the bad guys are still around?"

"I don't," Alexis assured her. "We need to be careful, just in case, but I think the guy probably had a temper tantrum over you spraying him with bear spray and decided to pay us back by tearing up our raft. They're probably long gone."

"And even if they aren't," Zeke told her, "these cabins aren't easy to find. You'll be safe here."

"You're sure?" Keira stared at him, daring him to lie.

"I'm sure." He met her eyes, and she nodded.

"Okay." Keira grinned. "In that case, what are we having for dinner?"

Alexis breathed a sigh of relief at Keira's easy acceptance of their situation. Funny that just yesterday Keira had been whining over missing a concert, but now, after being attacked and finding out they were stranded, she was handling it all with courage and maturity. "I'm so proud of you."

Keira looked surprised. "For what?"

"For being so strong and brave about this whole situation."

"Well, thanks." Keira gave a sly grin. "But you didn't answer my question about what's for dinner. Are you trying to change the subject?"

Zeke laughed. "I just fed you lunch an hour ago, kid. Are you hungry already?"

"Not really," Keira admitted. "But I'm a growing girl. I like to know where my next meal is coming from."

"I'm sure I can rustle up something. How do you feel about beans?"

Alexis put an arm around Keira's shoulders and squeezed. "Why don't Keira and I take care of dinner tonight?" If Zeke was willing to let them stay for several days, the least they could do was make themselves useful. "We have a fillet left from a Dolly Varden she caught yesterday, and we wouldn't want it to go to waste."

Zeke looked impressed. "You caught a Dolly, huh? Nice."

"It was a big one, too. I have a picture." Keira started to pull her phone from her pocket. "Oh, but the phone's dead."

"I'll take your word for it. I guess I'll get a little more work in on the cabin this afternoon, then, and look forward to a fine dinner tonight." Zeke collected his axe and saw and headed into the woods.

Alexis took the gear she'd collected to the small cabin with Keira trailing after her. She unpacked the food and pulled out the charger. "Here, Keira, if we put this charger in a sunny spot, we should be able to charge our phones in about five hours."

"You didn't tell me we had a phone charger! Oh, but we still won't be able to call without a signal."

"No, but you can take pictures, and we can use GPS to navigate."

"Yes, and I can play games! Let's get this charger charging!" Keira went outside, unfolded the plastic mat with its row of solar panels and laid it on a sunny rock. She pulled her phone from her pocket and plugged it into the USB cable. "Where's yours?"

Alexis dug her phone from her day pack and handed it over. "Here you go." She rummaged through her pack to verify that she was carrying a bandanna and a notepad. Once the phones were charged, she could get their GPS coordinates. And once their pickup date had passed and they'd been reported missing, she could set up a flag near the river at their campsite, along with GPS coordinates and directions to the cabin. Then all they would have to do was wait.

In the meantime, between the food they'd brought and the freeze-dried meals she always packed for emergencies, they could stay with Zeke without worrying they were eating up all his provisions. She had a sudden inspiration. "You know, I'd forgotten about it, but I saw some blueberries growing up in some of the alpine meadows. If we head uphill, we could probably find some for dinner."

"Ooh, that would be good."

After letting Zeke know where they were going and borrowing a bucket, they started up the hill. Keira still favored one leg, but it didn't seem to be slowing her down much. They hadn't even left the woods yet when Keira spotted some berries growing on creeping plants under the trees. "Are those blueberries?"

"No," Alexis said after looking closely. "But they're lowbush cranberries, which are really good, too. Go ahead and pick them."

Keira picked the six red berries from that plant and more from another one nearby. As they traveled uphill, she found several more cranberry plants, and by the time they reached the tree line, she'd gathered almost a cup.

Once they were in the sunshine, Alexis spotted a patch of the mossy-looking berry plants she was looking for growing nearby. When they got closer, they found the low shrubs bursting with ripe fruit. It must have been a particularly good year for blueberries, and fortunately, they'd discovered this patch before the grizzlies did.

Keira grabbed a handful and stuffed them in her mouth. "Testing," she mumbled.

"Of course." Alexis grinned. "Are they edible?"

"Not sure. I'd better try some more."

Alexis laughed and went to work filling the bucket with the deep blue fruits. Keira joined in, although only about half her berries fell into the bucket. The rest ended up in her mouth, which, along with her T-shirt, was turning purple from the berry juice. A fair number of Alexis's berries never hit the bucket, either. Still, they managed to collect a half bucketful and a few more cranberries on the way back to the cabins.

"Too bad we didn't have these when Zeke made pancakes this morning," Keira said. "I love blueberry pancakes. And muffins. And cake."

"I have instant oatmeal, brown sugar and butter. We could make a berry crumble for dessert tonight," Alexis suggested.

"Yes!"

While they'd been busy charging phones and picking berries, Zeke had cut, limbed and debarked another tree. He was in the clearing when they arrived, rolling the log to rest beside the cabin. He stopped to wipe the sweat from his forehead and waved. "Judging by the state of your shirt, I assume you were successful?" he called.

"Totally," Keira called back. "Just wait until dinner." She looked into the bucket. "I guess I should pick all these leaves out before we try to cook the berries."

"Why don't you work on that, and maybe see if you can get the berry juice out of your T-shirt if you don't want it stained forever. There's a bottle of camp suds in my pack and I saw that Zeke has a clothesline. I'll see if he needs any help with his work," Alexis told her. She crossed the clearing to where Zeke worked. "Anything I can help with?"

"That's okay. You're already doing dinner."

"Not for another couple of hours, and I'd love to understand more about the process of cabin building."

"If you're serious, I guess you can help me install this log."

"Sure. Just tell me what to do."

"Okay. Well, first I'll rough notch it." Using an axe, he cut a rough V about a foot from the end of the log. He then took a measuring tape from his pocket, marked the distance and chopped another rough V. "Now we need to set it in place."

She went to lift one end of the log while he lifted the other. It was heavy, especially when they had to lift it above their heads to set it in place at the top of the wall. "I can't believe you've been doing this alone," Alexis panted.

"It is a lot easier with your help." Zeke rotated the log slightly until the notches he'd cut rested securely on top of the logs below. He picked up a black iron tool that had been lying on the ground. It was about eight inches long, with a fork at one end bent at a right angle and a round handle at the other. A second piece with a sharp point like a pencil could slide up and down the body.

Zeke looked up and down the length of his log until he located the widest gap between the log they'd just added and the one below. He adjusted his tool until it matched the gap and moved it a little higher. Then he drew along the length of the lower log and around the joint, transferring the shape of the lower log onto the upper one by scratching it with the tool.

"You're creating a template here, so it fits flush with the log below?" Alexis asked.

"Exactly. But like I told you before, since I'm using green logs, I'm leaving an inch gap between each log to allow for twisting and settling as they dry. Want to help me lift it down?"

"Sure." Together they moved the log to the ground, where Zeke went to work with an axe and chisel, rounding out the notches and removing some wood from the bottom of the log until he was satisfied. They returned it to the wall, where it settled into place perfectly. "Amazing." Alexis sighted down the length of the log, at the perfectly even gap he'd left. "How did you make it so perfect, just from that one line?"

"Practice. At first, I'd have to fit the logs in place, carve out what I needed and try again. It would take four or five tries before it would fit properly. But I got better over time."

"I'll say." She picked up the tool. "This looks old."

"It is. I don't know how old. A neighbor found it in his grandfather's stuff and knew I liked this sort of thing, so he gave it to me. I didn't know what it was at first, but eventually I figured out it was a log scribe. That's when I got the idea of building a cabin like this. Immediately afterward, I happened to see an ad for this piece of land. And so I bought the land, read up on how to build a cabin and came out here."

"That's fascinating. So, you just gave up whatever you'd been doing before—"

"PT," he muttered.

"What's that?"

"I was a physical therapist." He spoke without looking at her.

"Impressive." Why give up that career to build a

cabin in the wild? Alexis tried to read his expression, but he wouldn't look her way. "It must have been rewarding work, helping people recover from injury."

He grunted something she didn't understand. "I'm going to go fell another tree. Call me when it's time to eat." And just like that, he shut her out. But not before she'd gotten another glimpse of his wounded soul.

"I'll pray for you," she called impulsively toward his back.

He slowed, but he didn't turn. After a moment, he answered, "You do that," and he walked away.

Chapter Six

Zeke slung the axe over his shoulder, grabbed his saw and marched into the forest to a straight spruce he'd already marked to be harvested. Working almost by rote, he identified the best path to fell the tree and cut a wedge in that side of the trunk with his axe. But all the while, his mind was churning. Why had he insisted Alexis and Keira stay with him while they waited for rescue? The whole point of him being here was to be alone. He wasn't supposed to be responsible for anyone else. He couldn't be.

Chop. Chips of spruce flew as his blade sank into the wood. Fragments of memory surfaced. The white wing struts on the Super Cub. The blur of the propeller. Chop. The clouds growing thicker. The turbulence. Chop. Dani, in the passenger seat, her lips moving in silent prayer. Chop. The mountainside suddenly visible through the clouds, too late—

Zeke dropped the axe, tilted back his head and

closed his eyes. He'd been arrogant, and Dani, his beloved Dani, had suffered and died because of it. Never again.

And now two more precious lives had been dropped on his doorstep. They shouldn't be here. There was too much to go wrong out here in the wilderness. They could get lost, run into bears, have an accident—and that didn't even take into account the men who had tried to snatch Keira and damaged the raft. Hopefully, they were gone, but how could Zeke be sure?

They needed to get out of here, back to where they would be safe. Just how damaged was the raft, anyway? Could it be repaired? Zeke gathered his axe and saw and returned to the cabins, where Alexis and Keira were busy peeling potatoes. The dog, napping on the porch, raised her head and wagged her tail at him. Yet another life he was responsible for. "I need to run down to the river," he told them. "Don't wait supper on me."

"But why—" Alexis asked.

Without answering or waiting for more questions, Zeke turned and jogged along the creek trail toward the river. It was time to see the damage to the raft himself.

Now, in August, the days were shorter than they had been at the solstice in June, but they were still getting around seventeen hours of daylight. The sky got dark at night now, not just the twilight between sunset and sunrise, but dark enough for stars. But he would be back at the cabin long before dark. He just needed to see what they were up against. He ran on.

Maybe Alexis was wrong. Maybe it was a bear that had damaged her raft. It was certainly understandable, after what had happened with Keira, that she might have leaped to the conclusion that the same people had vandalized her campsite.

He reached the river and turned upstream. He had to move more slowly now, as parts of the trail were covered with high water. As he traveled, he kept an eye out for signs that anyone had camped along the river recently, but he didn't see anything. Eventually, he spotted a blue tent set up on a rise, just off the river. He frowned. Alexis had mentioned damage, but other than a small rip in the rain fly, the tent was fine. So were the two sleeping bags, mats and a duffel full of clothes and personal items inside. He walked a little farther, past some bushes, and spotted the raft. Or at least, what was left of it.

The oar frame, made of sturdy metal pipes, sat unscathed on the inflated floor, but the blue tubes that formed the body of the boat had collapsed into piles. Zeke wasn't a rafting expert, but he had been on a few raft trips with friends. The material used for raft tubes was tough stuff. It didn't just collapse. On a boulder nearby, someone, presumably Alexis, had neatly stacked oars, bags, throw ropes and the other raft gear that would have been inside the raft. None of it appeared to be cut apart or damaged in any way.

So, what were the odds that a bear had come along, used his claws to rip each of the tubes apart, but not bothered with anything inside the boat, including the floor? On closer inspection, it was clearly a knife, not claws, that had severed the tubes. It looked like someone had first made a few random punctures and short slices, and then, perhaps impatient with the slow leaks, had slashed the length of each tube two or three times.

Alexis's theory was that the raft was destroyed in revenge for bear spray. But if anger was the motivation, wouldn't they have destroyed the items inside the raft as well, and probably the tent? And she said they'd stolen her satellite phone. Not destroyed, but stolen. And yet they'd left some expensive dry bags and camping equipment behind. Zeke wasn't liking the picture that was forming in his mind.

He moved upstream a hundred yards or so, to the wide beach and trailhead for Leah Falls. Judging from the lack of footprints in the mud at the base of the trail, no one had been there since the rain. Just upstream from there, the Pearson River became sandwiched between a bluff on one side and a marsh on the other. No one camped in a marsh, and he hadn't seen any sign of campers between here and the base of Serendipity Creek, which probably meant Keira's attackers had indeed powerboated down from Pearson Lake, and were almost certainly gone now. But there was nothing to prevent their return.

He needed to get back to the cabins. He might not want to be responsible for anyone else, but he was. Maybe this time he could do better. Be better. For the first time in a long time, he prayed aloud. "God, help me. Please. I don't know what I'm doing, but I have to keep them safe. Help me to listen to You, to follow Your guidance. Show me the way. Amen."

Was God listening to his prayers? Zeke wasn't sure. But one thing he was sure about. He was going to do everything in his power to protect the two precious souls who had wandered into his life. He turned downstream and started running.

They'd waited long past the usual time to cook dinner, but Zeke still hadn't returned by seven. Alexis was worried. Where had he gone so suddenly, and why? Was he okay? Had he discovered something or thought of some new danger she didn't know about? For Keira's sake, she tried to pretend this was normal activity, but inside she fretted.

"Will Zeke be back soon?" Keira asked, echoing her thoughts.

"I'm sure he will, and he'll be hungry after all that hard work. Let's go ahead and start cooking." She had Keira mix together the oatmeal, brown sugar and butter, and sprinkle it on top of the blueberries in the Dutch oven. Meanwhile, she took the potatoes they'd peeled earlier and left covered with water and cut them into thin slices.

"This is ready to go," Keira said.

"Okay." Alexis scraped coals from the fire to one side of the pit and arranged them in an even layer. "Set the Dutch oven on top, and then we'll put more coals on the lid. It should be ready in—" Alexis held her hand over the coals to judge how hot they were "—about forty-five minutes."

Keira, happy that her phone was now charged, took it from her pocket. "I'll set a timer."

"Good idea." Alexis thinly sliced onions, carrots and a lemon, added the potatoes, a fish fillet and a pat of butter, and wrapped the whole thing in the foil she'd brought. Then she repeated the process twice more. Once she had the packets ready to go, she set them on the grate over the fire. She considered waiting on Zeke until he came back, but the fish and veggies took time to cook and he would be hungry.

She was glad she did, because they'd just taken their dinner packets and the blueberry crumble off the fire when she spotted Zeke trotting up the trail. Keira called a greeting. He gave a little wave and walked over to the fire, carrying a familiar duffel bag.

"Thought you might want a change of clothes over the next couple days."

Clothes? He'd left her worrying about him while he went after something so trivial? "That's why you took off? To fetch clothes?"

He shrugged and held out the bag.

Alexis took it. As an example to Keira, she would remain polite. "Thank you. You're just in time for Keira's fish."

"Can't wait. I'm starving." He smiled at Keira when she handed him a plate with the biggest foil packet on top. "Yum. Thanks." He settled on the log.

Poppy, suck-up that she was, went to lean against his knee. He ran a hand over the dog's head.

Alexis's attitude softened as she watched him interact with the old dog. Keira sat down beside him and pulled out her phone. "Alexis brought a solar charger, so you can look at my pictures if you want."

"Let's see." Zeke set down his plate and leaned over the phone. He admired the fish photo and continued to ooh and aah over all the pictures Keira had snapped on their way down the river the first day. "That's a really nice one of Denali. You don't catch it without clouds too often."

"I know. And look." Keira pointed at a speck on the sky. "There's an eagle, too."

"That's great. You'll have to get it enlarged and framed once you get home," he told her.

Any remaining annoyance Alexis was feeling evaporated. She could see what he was doing, reaffirming to Keira that she would, indeed, be going home again. Delaying his meal to give her the kind of attention her own father never seemed to find time for. Zeke Soto was a generous man.

Funny how rare this sort of generosity of time was in the world today. Dixon bought Keira pretty much anything she asked for, but he couldn't seem to spare five minutes of undivided attention for his daughter. Most of the men Alexis had dated were the same: kind, willing to pitch in, but so caught up in their busy lives they never really gave anyone their undivided attention. Multitasking was the norm. Maybe that was just how life was these days, and Alexis was fooling herself to think it could be different. Unrealistic expectations could be the reason she was still single at thirty-three.

But here was Zeke. With no technology, no appliances, no vehicles, he worked from dawn to dusk just building his cabin and subsisting. And yet he took the time to really listen to Keira's thoughts. While Keira hunted for another photo on the phone, Zeke looked up at Alexis, and she smiled at him. He smiled back, a genuine smile that warmed her like a hug.

"Maybe we should let Zeke eat while the food is hot and look at pictures later," Alexis suggested.

"Oh, yeah." Keira put her phone in her pocket and picked up her own plate.

Zeke cleared his throat. "Is it all right if I say grace tonight?"

"Please do," Alexis replied.

He bowed his head and closed his eyes. "Our Lord, we thank You for the bounty of this earth, for the fish and the berries and all the good things. And I thank You for Keira and Alexis and their hard work catching and preparing the food. Please watch over them and keep them safe. Amen."

"Amen." Alexis watched as Zeke opened his foil packet and inhaled the lemon-scented steam. "Wow, pretty fancy cuisine for a man who's been living off beans and stew."

"Don't you fish?" Keira asked.

"I do, although I haven't made it down in a couple weeks." He took a bite. "This is so good. Have the silvers made it up Pearson River this far yet?"

"I saw a few, but I didn't catch any," Alexis told him. "I suspect there will be more by now. Maybe tomorrow Keira and I can fish, and if we catch some, you can give smoke-dried salmon another try."

"Good idea. The batch Poppy has been eating is made from chum salmon, so that might have been part of the problem. I'll come fishing with you."

"Don't you need to work on your cabin?"

"I can skip a day occasionally. That's a good idea to preserve some fish for later. Tell me how you made these packets."

The easy conversation continued over dinner, but occasionally Alexis would catch Zeke scanning the woods around them, as though he expected danger. Had he found evidence of the men from Leah Falls on his trip down to the river? She would have to question him later if she could find a minute alone with him. He raved over the blueberry dessert, praising Keira's campfire cooking skills until her cheeks turned pink.

As soon as he'd finished his dessert, but before he could get up to start cleaning, Keira's phone was out again. "Here's one of my favorite pictures. It's me, Alexis, and my best friends, Elise and Sarah, on Flattop on summer solstice last summer. We didn't do it this year, because I was spending the night with Elise, and her mom wouldn't take us."

"Last year's solstice on Flattop?" Zeke's face

changed, like he was bracing himself for something. "I was there, too."

"That's cool! There are some people in the crowd behind us. Maybe you're in the picture, too." She expanded the photo and shook her head. "No, nobody with a beard like yours." She handed him the phone.

When he looked at the picture, his face seemed to pale. Keira didn't notice, though, and after a moment he smiled and handed the phone back. "Good shot of all of you."

"May I see?" Alexis asked. She was familiar with the picture. In fact, she had a copy on her fireplace mantel, but she wanted to see what had thrown Zeke. Keira was right—there was no one with a beard in the background, but there was a clean-shaven man with familiar brown eyes, and he had an arm around a pretty blonde woman who was looking up at him adoringly.

What happened? How had he gone from a man in love to one living alone in a log cabin? What went wrong? Alexis returned the phone. "We'd better get this cleaned up. Keira, could you feed Poppy, please? I left her kibble in the cabin."

"Okay. Come on, Poppy." They trotted off.

Alexis took Zeke's plate. She would have liked to ask about the woman in the picture, but if he'd wanted to talk about her, he would have said something. Instead, she asked, "What did you find down there?"

"Where?"

"At my campsite down by the river. Something's wrong. I can tell."

He shook his head. "Nothing you don't already know about. But I saw what they did to your raft. Vicious, the way they ripped it apart."

"Yes." It was vicious, done by someone with a nasty temper. "I thank God that Keira had the presence of mind to use her bear spray and get away from them. But they're gone now. We'll be okay until a rescue party arrives."

"I'll keep you safe." Zeke spoke as if saying the words aloud would make them true.

The dots connected. "That's why you said you'd go fishing with us tomorrow. To keep us safe."

Zeke shrugged and added more wood to the fire under the pot of water Alexis was heating to wash up.

"You don't have to babysit us."

"Maybe not." He met her eyes. "But if anything happened to you or Keira, I wouldn't be able to face myself in the mirror."

She had to admit, she felt a lot safer when he was around. And she had Keira to consider. "Okay. But we don't have to fish if you need to be building. We can help you here."

"No, fishing is a good idea. I can keep building on into fall and winter, but I can only catch salmon during their migration. It will be good."

She laid a hand on his arm and looked into those kind brown eyes. "Thank you, Zeke."

"No problem." He busied himself with the fire.

And she thanked God once again that they'd stumbled upon Zeke's cabin.

Chapter Seven

The next morning after breakfast, they gathered their equipment. Alexis had topped up the phones with the solar charger while they prepared breakfast and ate. They filled water bottles with boiled and cooled water, and Alexis packed her portable UV water purifier in her day pack. She wasn't going to be caught without usable drinking water again. She'd left their fishing equipment in camp, so they had a long hike in front of them.

While Zeke was putting out the fire, Keira played with her phone. "Did you say you can use the GPS even when you don't have a cell signal?" she asked Alexis.

"Yes. I plan to write down our GPS coordinates here at the cabin and leave them at the campsite so that rescuers can find us more easily."

"How do you find GPS coordinates?"

"It's built in to your phone. Let me show you."

Alexis pulled up the preinstalled mapping app and zoomed in to show more detail. "See, it says we're right here. You just have to drop a pin by holding down your finger and the coordinates pop up on the top here. Then you can save or share those coordinates with other people."

"So, like, if Elise and I are at the state fair and we get separated, I can send her a pin and she can find me with her phone?"

"Exactly."

"Cool."

"Yeah, technology is great."

A soft chuckle indicated that Zeke had overheard. She grinned at him. Technology was great, although she respected the historic craftsmanship he preferred as well.

"Are you going to leave a note with the coordinates at the campsite today?" Keira asked.

"That's a good idea." Alexis had planned to wait until the day they were due to meet the plane at Chapel Lake, but since they were going to camp today, she might as well save herself a trip. "In fact, now that I think about it, that's a really good idea. If other rafters or kayakers come down the river and see our distress signal, they might have a satellite phone to call in a rescue for us right away." She dropped a pin on her phone, but also jotted down the coordinates, along with written directions, onto the notepad she always carried.

"Ready?" she asked Zeke.

He'd been busy adjusting something in his pack, but now he nodded and shrugged it onto his shoulders. "All set."

The four of them headed down to the river. Zeke led the way, carrying his fly rod. Alexis brought up the rear, where she could keep an eye on Keira and Poppy. All traces of Keira's limp had disappeared, and the scrapes on her knee were healing nicely. The can of bear spray was still there on her belt. Some instinct must have warned her to return it to the holster before she'd run. Alexis touched her own can of bear spray on one hip and her .44 on the other. She told herself it was in case of bears, but if she were honest, it was more than that.

Last evening when they were all sitting around the fire, safe and secure, fishing had sounded like an excellent idea. But today, taking Keira away from the cabins felt scary. Maybe it was because the Pearson River was the point where boaters and rafters could access the area. It felt a little like when Alexis was a kid playing capture the flag, and she left her own "safe" territory to run for the opponent's flag. But she hadn't seen any sign of anyone else camping along the river and neither had Zeke. It would be fine. All the same, she was glad Zeke had chosen to come along.

When they reached the river, she saw that the water level had dropped some since she'd been there before. That was good news, both because it would make for better fishing and because it meant the game trail that ran along the bank, while still muddy, would be passable. By the time they made it to the campsite without any sign of other people on the river, Alexis had relaxed. She collected their fishing equipment. "Do you want to fish here or move upstream?" she asked Zeke.

"We can start here. That pool across the river looks promising."

She grinned. "That's what I thought, but I didn't catch anything when I fished it two days ago."

He winked. "Maybe you didn't have the right fly."

"Let me guess. You hand tie all your fishing flies using only feathers and fur from native species."

He chuckled. "More or less. But I confess, I bought this fly rod and reel from Anchorage Fishing Supply last summer."

"Yeah, the PVC-covered Dacron fly line isn't exactly historic, either," Alexis pointed out.

"Are you guys going to talk all day, or are we going to fish?" Keira demanded.

Alexis tied a spoon onto the line of Keira's spinning rod and handed it over. "Here. Go catch something."

"Aye, aye." Keira gave a mock salute and went to cast her line into the river.

Alexis wriggled into her chest waders and fastened the belt. While Zeke did the same, she tied her favorite wet fly onto her line and tried to peek at his, but she couldn't get a good look. Once he was ready, she suggested, "Last one to catch a silver has to clean the fish?"

"You're on. But I'm fishing that pool."

"Me, too. I'll give you first cast."

They both waded into the water, Alexis fifteen yards or so upriver from Zeke. He cast, his line expertly looping over the water and setting the tip at the edge of the pool. He let it drift past any salmon who might be resting there. His line wiggled, and for a moment Alexis thought she'd lost the contest without ever casting a line, but whatever fish had toyed with it decided to pass. He pulled in his line, and it was Alexis's turn.

She cast, landing her fly just upstream of the pool to give it a moment to sink to the proper depth before it reached the fish. Seconds later, she felt a little tug and set the hook. "Fish on."

"Go, Alexis!" Keira called. "Girl power!"

Alexis laughed and played the fish closer. "Feels like a big one."

"I'll get the net," Keira offered.

"And I'll get my fillet knife," Zeke said. "Well done."

"It's not landed yet." Alexis didn't want to get ahead of herself. The fish was putting up a fight, but neither Zeke nor Keira seemed worried. Eventually Alexis managed to work it into the shallow water at the shoreline where Keira could scoop it up in the net.

"It's a silver all right, and nickel bright," Zeke declared. "Good eating." He waited until Alexis had removed the hook. "May I see what fly you're using, or is it a secret?"

"Take a look."

He examined the fly and laughed. "A golden hare's ear. How about that?" He showed her the almost-identical fly on the end of his line. "I didn't know anyone used these anymore."

"It was one of my dad's favorites. A little old-fashioned, but I figure fish are still fish, and they still eat mayflies, so why wouldn't the fly still work?"

Zeke chuckled. "Well, since we were both using the same fly and yours got a strike, I guess we know who's the better fisherperson."

"I doubt that. But since we haven't caught our limit and you're doing all the cleaning, we might as well keep fishing. Right, Keira?"

"Right!" Keira picked up her rod and cast again.

By noon, Zeke had pulled in another silver and Keira had hooked a nice grayling, but she'd decided to release it. Zeke cleaned the salmon, leaving the two sides joined at the tail, and slipped the fillets into gallon-sized plastic bags Alexis provided. A Steller's jay landed in a tree nearby and watched Zeke work, looking for an opportunity to swoop in and grab lunch. Sunshine reflected off the almost-iridescent feathers of the bird's head and chest. Keira pulled out her phone and crept closer, trying to snap a good picture.

Poppy lay sprawled out on the bank, snoozing in

the sun. Zeke packed the fish into his backpack and slung it over his shoulders. "Good fishing day. I'm looking forward to starting the brining and smoking process. Are you ready to head home?"

"Just let me set up this flag and note." Alexis pulled the bandanna from her day pack and looked for a suitable tree limb that would be highly visible to anyone on the river.

"What's this?" Zeke asked.

"I'm leaving a note with the GPS coordinates for the cabin so that rescuers can find us," Alexis explained.

Zeke glanced at Keira, who was still busy with the bird, and then back at Alexis. "Is that a good idea?" he asked in a low voice. "You said they won't even start looking for another four days."

"Yes, but once the main salmon run hits Chapel Lake and the word gets out, there will be plenty of boaters on the river. My note asks anyone who finds it to alert a rescue crew as soon as possible. The sooner I can get Keira home, the better."

"Okay," Zeke said slowly. "I guess that makes sense."

She laid a hand on his arm. "Thank you, Zeke, for coming fishing with us today. I confess, I feel a whole lot safer with you around. I thank God for leading us to your cabin two days ago."

An expression she couldn't quite identify crossed his face. "You think God led you to me?"

"I do."

He shook his head but smiled at the same time. "I love the way you say 'I do' like it's completely self-evident. No doubts."

"I have doubts about a lot of things," Alexis told him, "but this isn't one of them. From what you say, you're the only one living anywhere in the area. The odds of us finding you—"

"You said you were following the creek."

"Yes, but we'd already crossed a couple of other creeks. I believe God led us to follow that one, and He led us to you." Those beautiful green eyes of hers looked directly into his. "You don't agree?"

"Maybe." Zeke took a deep breath. "Or maybe it's all coincidence. I don't know. To be honest, I'm not too in tune with God's plans right now, but it's hard to imagine He would send you to me, of all people."

"Why would you say that?" she asked.

"Well, I don't want to get into it, but my track record hasn't been the best."

"Well, I believe in a loving God who watches over us," Alexis told him. "And God believes in you."

"I'm sooooo hungry." Predictably, the minute they were in sight of the cabins, Keira's stomach demanded food. Zeke looked up at the position of the sun. It was a little late for lunch, he supposed.

"I've got some freeze-dried meals I can get done fast," Alexis suggested. "What kind do you want, Zeke? I think I've got chili mac, chicken teriyaki, spaghetti—"

"Anything is fine," he told her. "I'll start some water

boiling and then get on those fish fillets." Keira was still debating between chicken teriyaki and lasagna as he walked away.

He prepared the salmon fillets for smoking by slashing them crosswise several times for maximum surface area and coating them with a mixture of salt and sugar. He spread them on a grate to dry. By the time they'd finished lunch and cleaned up, it would be time to brush off the salt and allow a pellicle to form before hanging the fish on wooden racks over a smoky fire. Once the fish were completely dried and smoked, they would last without refrigeration all winter. At least, that was the theory.

He looked back toward the fire. Keira was holding a food pouch open while Alexis poured boiling water inside. The old yellow Lab stood nearby, ready in case anyone should drop a crumb. Keira said something and Alexis laughed, that wonderful, musical laugh that made everyone in the vicinity smile. At least, that was the effect it had on him.

She was amazing, this woman. Loving. Caring. Strong in body, but even stronger in spirit. And in faith. *God believes in you.* That was what she'd told him, back at the river. Could it be true? But why would God believe in him, after he'd failed so spectacularly? Dani had trusted Zeke with her life, and she'd paid with it. If Alexis knew his history, she wouldn't be so ready to trust.

God knew the truth. And yet, according to Alexis, God had led them right to Zeke. Maybe he was the only man available for the job. But what if he failed again? What if he couldn't keep them safe? The danger seemed to have left the area, but Zeke wouldn't rest easy until they were on a plane back to Anchorage. *I'll do my best, Lord. I promise.*

"Zeke! Your gourmet lunch awaits," Alexis called.

"Be right there." He washed his hands in the creek and went to join the others. As soon as he arrived, Keira, obviously impatient to eat, recited a quick prayer, opened her pouch, and poured her rice and chicken onto a plate.

Alexis handed him a bowl of chili mac. "I'll help you with the cabin this afternoon," she offered.

"You don't have to."

"I want to. I'm fascinated by the way you can lock the logs together at the corners and they stay in place with no nails or fasteners."

"There's a log cabin still standing in New Jersey that was built in 1638," he told her. "I came across an article when I was researching cabin-building techniques."

"Wow. I wonder if your cabin will still be around in almost four hundred years. My house won't be."

"I like your house." Keira turned to Zeke. "She designed it herself."

"Really?" Zeke wondered what sort of home Alexis would design. A farmhouse? An A-frame? Or something cutting-edge and modern? "Tell me about it."

"It's small," Alexis told him. "About seventeen

hundred square feet. Of course, compared to this cabin—" she pointed to the one they'd been sleeping in "—that's huge. It's kind of a modern take on a cottage, with exposed beams and a fireplace, but with high ceilings, lots of light and open space."

"The roof doesn't match," Keira said.

"She means the two gables don't meet at the top. Instead, I have a row of south-facing clerestory windows along the higher side to let light deep into the house."

"That sounds really nice."

"Thank you. I like it."

He could imagine a home Alexis would design. Beautiful but practical. Warm and welcoming. Much like the woman sitting across the fire from him right now. A woman who could make anyone in her presence feel like they were home.

Bed felt good that night. After fishing all morning, Alexis had assisted Zeke in making a second firepit a little distance from the cabins and assembling a rack to hang the salmon on while they smoked. Zeke had plenty of green alder to burn, left from clearing the area to build his cabins. Once they had the fish hung and the smoky fire going, they'd left Keira in charge of feeding the fire while the two of them worked on the cabin.

Together, they'd been able to get three logs scribed and installed. Zeke said having an extra pair of hands was a great help in setting those high logs into place, which made Alexis feel less guilty about the time he'd taken off to go fishing with them. Or more accurately, to guard them while they fished. But at least he'd gotten some nice salmon out of the deal.

Keira was already asleep. She'd gone inside while Alexis was still brushing her teeth and banking the fire and must have dropped off practically the moment her head hit the rolled-up fleece jacket she was using as a pillow. Poppy snored softly from under the bunk. But Alexis couldn't hear a sound from Zeke's direction.

"Zeke?" she whispered. "Are you awake?"

"Uh-huh." His soft voice came from the dark. "You okay?"

"I'm fine. I just wanted to say thank you. Today was a good day."

"I should be thanking you. You caught a bunch of fish for me, and I got a lot more done on the cabin than I ever could have alone."

"It was fun."

"Not many women would say that."

"They don't know what they're missing. Anyway, good night, Zeke."

"Good night, Alexis. Sleep well."

She did sleep well, until sometime in the darkness, she was awakened by Poppy's frantic barking. The little bit of moonlight from the small opening near the eaves enabled her to make out Zeke's form next to the door.

"Poppy, hush." The dog quit barking, but she whimpered. "What is it?" Alexis asked Zeke.

"Not sure yet, but it could be that the smoking salmon attracted a bear." He finished loading both barrels of his shotgun and clicked it into place. "I'll check it out."

"Be careful." She sent up a silent prayer as he lifted the wooden latch and slipped out the door.

"What's going on?" Keira was awake, too.

"Poppy was barking at something. Zeke thinks it might be a bear." Alexis slipped out of bed and reached for her revolver. "Stay here and latch the door behind me."

"Don't leave me." Keira grabbed for her shoulder.

Alexis was dying to see what was going on outside, but she wouldn't desert Keira if she was afraid. "Okay, I won't. I'm just going to peek out the door, then. You hold Poppy's collar, all right?"

"All right." Keira grabbed the dog.

Alexis slipped across the cabin and looked out. Zeke was standing nearby, clearly visible in the moonlight, shotgun at the ready. A dark shape ran from the shadow of the half-built cabin into the woods, crashing through some brush. Alexis got a glimpse of something reflective, and then it was gone.

Sometimes animal eyes shone in the dark like that, but this reflection looked more like those stripes that were sometimes added to shoes to make pedestrians more visible at dusk. "It wasn't a bear, was it?" she whispered to Zeke.

"Don't think so."

She sucked in a breath as the realization hit. "Oh, no. By leaving the GPS information at camp, I led the bad guys right to us." She slapped her forehead. "Stupid."

"You don't know that," Zeke answered.

"A rescuer wouldn't be prowling around in the middle of the night, and if he was, he would have identified himself."

"Whoever it was, he's gone now," Zeke told her. "Let's get inside." He came in and latched the door behind him. "I doubt anyone will be back tonight," he said in a soothing voice. "Let's all try to get some sleep."

Like that was going to happen. But they needed to reassure Keira. "You're right. We need rest." Alexis tucked Keira in and lay beside her, staring at the dark ceiling. Tomorrow she would retrieve that note with their coordinates. But all they could do tonight was wait and hope the intruder didn't return.

Chapter Eight

Alexis doubted that any of them even closed their eyes for the rest of the night, but Keira finally fell asleep about five thirty, just as the sun made an appearance. Zeke quietly slipped out the door, with Poppy right behind him. Alexis decided to follow, carrying her shoes. She sat down on the front steps to put them on. A minute later, Zeke returned, carrying a bucket and pot full of water.

"She still asleep?" he asked, quietly.

Alexis nodded. "We might as well let her rest." She finished tying her laces and moved over to the fire ring, where she added some wood to build up the flames before placing the grate in place so that Zeke could heat the water.

He nodded his thanks and set a big pot on to boil. She held out the coffeepot and he filled it from the second bucket. She set it on the grate beside the pot. After three days together, she'd begun to learn the routine. Boiled water for drinking and coffee, and then another pot for washing.

"Did you check on the salmon?" she asked, oddly reluctant to bring up the topic of last night's prowler. For just a moment, she wanted to pretend everything was the same as yesterday.

"It's looking good. I added more wood to the fire. Didn't see any fresh tracks around it."

"So you don't think it was a bear last night."

He looked at her and lifted an eyebrow. "No."

"I thought I saw what looked like reflective tape from a shoe when whatever it was ran into the woods. Did you?"

He nodded, destroying her hope that she'd misinterpreted what she saw. "It was a man. I found a footprint at the edge of the woods."

"You don't seem all that surprised. We didn't see any signs of people when we were at the river yesterday."

"No. But—" He paused while he added grounds to the coffeepot.

"But what? Did you think they would be back?"

"I just—" He returned the pot to the fire. "We were working under the theory that whoever tried to nab Keira also destroyed your raft in a fit of spite."

"Are you saying you think it was different people? It's hard to believe there were two sets of criminals wandering around Leah Falls that one day."

"No, I don't think there were two sets of criminals. But didn't you notice anything odd about the damage?"

"Like what?"

"Like the tent and the equipment. They ripped your boat to pieces and took your phone, but you had some expensive dry bags they could have stolen or destroyed. Your tent campsite looked untouched. If they were trying to harm you, wouldn't they have damaged the tent?"

She nodded slowly. "So you think it was deliberate. The damage to the raft wasn't revenge—it was a strategic attempt to keep us here."

"I think so."

"Why didn't you say anything? Especially when I told you I was leaving a note telling people how to find us."

"I should have." He took a deep breath and turned to meet her eyes. "I'm sorry."

"But why didn't you?" she demanded.

"I guess I didn't want it to be true. We'd seen no sign of anyone on the river. I thought I was wrong. And your idea of signaling any raft groups that might pass by made sense. I thought it was worth the risk."

"You still should have told me your theory and let me make the decision."

"You're right. I promise, if I have any suspicions from here on out, I'll voice them. I am sorry." He looked so contrite, she had to smile.

"I'm sorry, too. None of this is your fault. I'm just upset that I brought Keira into this situation."

She huffed in frustration. "This was supposed to be a healing trip, and instead I've put her into danger."

"What do you mean, a healing trip?" He poured a cup of coffee from the pot and handed it to her before pouring one for himself.

"Thanks." She set the cup down to cool for a moment. "Keira's at a tough age. She's starting middle school later this month, and the situation between her parents isn't helping."

"She mentioned that she was supposed to be with her father this week, but he had to go out of town."

"That's right. I wish I could say that was a rare occurrence, but it's not. Dixon is consumed with growing the company. It's so different from the way it was when I was Keira's age, and my dad was in charge. He deliberately kept the company small, so that he could actively participate in some of the tours. I used to tag along all the time, helping where I could and learning the ropes. Being outdoors, challenging myself—it made a huge difference in my life."

"You were close to your dad?"

"Yes. Especially after my mother died when I was fifteen. By the time I was a junior in high school and Dixon was in college, we were taking out raft tours on our own in the summer. Dixon joined Dad in Mahoney Tours when he graduated with a business degree. I'd planned to do the same, but my freshman calculus professor pulled me aside one day and asked if I'd ever considered engineering. I've always been fascinated with the nuts and bolts of buildings, so with my dad's blessing, I changed majors."

"From what you've told me about your work, you made the right decision. Was your father disappointed?"

"Maybe a little, but he said God had given me certain gifts, and it was my job to use them well. He'd set up a system where every year Dixon worked for him, he earned a small share of the company. At the end of my sophomore year of college, Dad died and Dixon took over. At that point, the ten percent Dixon already owned plus the forty-five percent he inherited made him majority owner. He wanted to borrow money to expand the company. I wasn't comfortable with that. So he bought out my share as well."

"I gather his plan was successful."

"Very. But it cost him his marriage, and if he's not careful, it might cost him his relationship with his daughter."

"Do you regret selling out to him?"

"Not at all. That money covered the cost of my education, and after I'd worked six years and earned my professional engineer certification, it allowed me to start my own business on my own terms. I'm blessed." She took a sip of coffee. "Now, Keira's mom, on the other hand, would disagree."

"Oh?"

"She and Dixon divorced about a year after he took over the company. The part he inherited wasn't marital property, but she was entitled to half of the ten percent he owned when Dad died. He bought her out, based on the appraised value of the company at that time. Keep in mind, he'd just borrowed a ton of money and the investments hadn't yet begun to pay off. The company is probably worth ten times today what it was when they divorced. Mara is convinced he cheated her, and she goes out of her way to make things difficult for him, including pointing out all his faults to his daughter on every occasion."

"Sounds toxic."

"That's an accurate description. It puts Keira in the position of either having to defend her father or seeming to agree with her mother. And Dixon doesn't help matters. He's always buying Keira stuff, when what she needs is his time."

"And your role in all this?"

"I'm just the aunt. I try to keep on Mara's good side, so she'll let me spend time with Keira. Same with Dixon. I attempt to nudge him into spending more time with Keira without making myself so obnoxious he avoids me."

Zeke laughed. "I can't imagine you ever being obnoxious."

"Well, thanks, but I confess, the temptation is there to tell my brother he's being very foolish." She sipped her coffee. "And speaking of obnoxious, here I am, laying all my family's troubles on you, when I've already dragged you into a scary situation. I'm sorry."

"Don't be sorry. I'm honored you trust me with

your family secrets." Zeke topped off his coffee and hers before settling back on the log. "In fact, maybe the two are related."

"What do you mean?"

"Keira's father is a wealthy man. What if this wasn't a random attack?"

"You mean—"

"What if they were trying to kidnap Keira and hold her for ransom?"

Ransom? Could it be? Alexis knew Dixon had grown the company to the point where he was worth a lot of money, but she'd never considered his success might make Keira a target. But the Mahoney name was out there, on the sides of the buses, on lodges and hotels, on television and radio ads. It might have given someone ideas. "It would explain why, as you said, they disabled the raft but not the camping gear."

"Who would have known you were taking Keira here?"

"Not many people." She ticked off on her fingers. "Her parents, of course. My assistant, whom I would trust with my life. I probably mentioned it to a few friends at church. And of course, there's the flying service that dropped us at Pearson Lake and is scheduled to pick us up at Chapel Lake in a few days. I guess more than I realized."

"Not to mention, any of those people might have told their friends and family, who told theirs, and so on."

"So, it could have been anyone."

"Or I might be totally off base," Zeke admitted. "This may have nothing to do with Mahoney Tours."

"I suppose it doesn't really matter why they're doing this," Alexis mused. "The important thing is keeping Keira safe."

"True."

Alexis pressed her fingers to her forehead and shook her head. "I can't believe I left a note leading them here. Endangering all of us."

Zeke sipped his coffee, a thoughtful look on his face. "It's possible the note had nothing to do with it. Someone might have been wandering around, smelled the fish smoking and went to check it out, just like the bears we were worried about."

"In the middle of the night?"

"Possibly. Whoever it was didn't try to break in. We just knew about them because the dog barked. Maybe it was a different person than whoever destroyed your raft."

Alexis set her coffee cup on the ground and stood up. "If that's the case, I should retrieve the note I left yesterday in case the kidnappers do come back and find it."

Zeke shook his head. "I don't think you should go in case last night's prowler is involved."

"Why not? Keira can stay here with you, where she'll be safe."

"But you wouldn't be."

"Why would kidnappers be after me?"

"If they can't get your brother's daughter, they might decide his sister would do just as well."

"I never thought of that." Alexis paced beside the fire. "But if they don't already know where we are, I hate the thought of that note sitting there, acting like a compass."

"I'll go." Zeke finished the last of his coffee and set the cup on the log beside him. "If I run, I can be there and back in a little over two hours."

"Are you sure?"

"Yeah. But—" He gave her a stern look. "I want you, Keira and Poppy to stay inside the cabin while I'm gone."

"Gone where?" Keira was on the front steps, rubbing her eyes. Poppy wandered over to press her head against Keira's leg, and she rested her hand on the dog's head.

"After last night's prowler, I've decided it was a bad idea to leave instructions at the river for anyone to find," Alexis admitted to Keira. "Zeke is going to get them back."

"But if they already know where we are—"

"Maybe they do, or maybe they don't," Zeke told her. "But I, for one, will feel better if there's no signpost showing everyone exactly where to find you."

"Zeke thinks we should stay inside while he's gone," Alexis told her. "And I agree with him. So, the water is boiling. Let's make some oatmeal for breakfast and we can get this done. In fact, I'll make an extra bucket of warm water, and we can use the time inside the cabin to wash our hair while Zeke's gone." That should keep Keira occupied for a while. "Okay?"

Keira opened her mouth as though to argue, but she seemed to think better of it. "Okay."

"Come here." Alexis opened her arms and pulled Keira into a hug. "We're going to be fine. God will see us through."

"I know this one. The US paid Russia seven point two million to purchase Alaska."

"Correct." Alexis watched Keira move her marker on the tiny folding game board into the last square.

"I win!" Keira cheered.

"It's been too long since I studied all this in school," Alexis grumbled. She was glad she'd thought to bring the trivia game along. It had made for a welcome distraction while they waited. She and Keira had left their phones outside plugged into the solar charger, so she had no way of knowing, but she suspected Zeke had been gone less than an hour, although it seemed like forever.

They'd already taken turns washing each other's hair and she'd arranged Keira's into a French braid down her back. She mixed the cards they hadn't used yet and passed the stack to Keira. Keira took the top card, but instead of reading the question, she asked, "How long do you think Zeke will be gone?"

"He said he should be able to run there and back in about two hours."

"Do you think he'll be okay?"

Alexis nodded. "Zeke can take care of himself. And as far as I know, nobody wants to mess with him."

"Why do they want us?" Keira asked in a small voice.

"I don't know for sure," Alexis answered, weighing how much to tell her. She decided honesty was the best policy. "But Zeke thinks someone might be trying to kidnap you for ransom."

"Ransom?" Keira seemed as surprised by the thought as Alexis had been.

"Don't worry. We're not going to let that happen."

"Do you think whoever was outside last night was one of the kidnappers?"

"Maybe. We just don't know. That's why Zeke went to retrieve the note I left."

"But what if the rescuers come and can't find us?"

"They'll keep looking. Your dad won't let them give up on us." Alexis nodded at the card in Keira's hand. "What are my category choices?"

"Alaska state history for ten points or favorites for five."

"I'll try favorites."

"What is the official state mineral of Alaska?"

"Oh, I've got this one. Jade."

"Wrong! Jade is the official state gemstone. The official state mineral is gold."

"Of course." Alexis slapped her forehead. "I knew that."

Keira was winning yet another game when Poppy suddenly jumped up and let out a woof.

They both froze, staring at each other. It could be Zeke, but he wouldn't have had time to get all the way to the campsite and back yet. Alexis double-checked to make sure the heavy wooden bar was in place to hold the door secure. Footsteps sounded on the steps outside. Keira's eyes went wide. Alexis raised her finger to her lips and motioned for Keira to move to the corner of the cabin where she would be hidden if the door swung inward.

Someone knocked on the door. A pleasant male voice called, "Hello. Anyone home? I'm from Search and Rescue."

It was too soon. No one knew they were missing yet. Unless—someone in a powerboat from Pearson Lake could have seen their camp deserted and called it in. But what if it was the kidnappers? She looked over at Keira, who was peering through the gaps between the logs where the chinking had fallen out in the saggy corner. Poppy was there, too, sniffing. She wasn't barking, but a low grumbling growl emanated from her throat. Keira looked over and shook her head, violently. Maybe she recognized the man.

He tried the door, and finding it latched, he shook it several times. "Ma'am, could you open the door, please? I'm a volunteer from up at Pearson Lake. **We're looking for Alexis and Keira Mahoney. Someone reported a request for rescue on a note left at the river."**

Definitely not Search and Rescue. Alexis had put her name on the note, but she hadn't mentioned Keira. And how would he know there was a "ma'am" inside the cabin unless he'd been watching them, waiting for Zeke to leave? Then she remembered— Keira's shirt on the clothesline. If he'd seen Zeke leave, he'd know there was a woman left behind.

Now the man knocked again, harder. "Anyone there? If you're injured, stay back from the door. I'll break in."

Alexis swallowed. The heavy wooden bar wouldn't break easily, but it wouldn't be hard for him to find Zeke's axes. She cleared her throat and tried to add about fifty years to her voice. "Go 'way. You're trespassing. I don't know any Mahoneys and there ain't nobody 'round here but me."

"Who is this?" the man called through the door.

"Ain't none of your business," Alexis rasped, "but I've got me a shotgun here, and if you don't get off my land real soon, you're gonna wish you had."

"Have you seen a woman and a girl wandering around here—"

"Git out!"

"I'm going." Footsteps sounded on the steps.

Alexis joined Keira in the corner, where they could see someone's lower legs, encased in hiking pants, and orange hiking boots. Just like the orange boots she'd spotted in the forest that first day. And these boots appeared to have reflective stripes along the sides.

Clearly, it had been a waste of time sending Zeke after the note. The kidnappers had found it and it brought them right here. Alexis didn't fool herself that the man had believed she wasn't Alexis Mahoney. He was just biding his time, working out a plan to get at them. The real search-and-rescue teams wouldn't even be looking for Keira and her for another three days. They had to get out of here.

But without a raft, how could they?

Chapter Nine

Zeke jogged into the campsite. At first glance, everything seemed the same, but when he went to retrieve Alexis's bandanna flag and note, they were gone. A blurred footprint nearby that was too big to be Alexis's or Keira's and didn't match his own boots confirmed that they hadn't been removed by accident. Which meant the kidnappers knew exactly where to find Keira and Alexis. He should never have left them alone!

He turned back and ran along the river path faster than he'd ever moved before. He was almost to the creek that led up to his cabin when he heard it—the sound of a motorboat coming up the river. If the kidnappers already had Keira and Alexis, they would be bringing them to the boat. He ducked behind a spruce tree while the boat passed him, and a few minutes later, the engine sounds stopped. They must be waiting at the mouth of the creek. He moved closer, staying out of sight, until he could see the boat. Just one man sat waiting, a big strong guy with a hat pulled low over his eyes and his face covered by a fabric buff.

Zeke circled around noiselessly so that he could see up the trail. No sign of them yet. Assuming there were still only two kidnappers, Zeke might be able to surprise the other one and get Alexis and Keira away from him before he knew what was happening. It was worth a try. He moved up the trail, far enough away so that the man waiting in the boat wouldn't hear and render aid.

The next hour must have been the longest in his life, but eventually Zeke heard footsteps on the trail. It didn't sound like three people, though. A few minutes later, a man wearing a gray T-shirt and hiking pants hurried by. Zeke couldn't see his face from this angle, but his slim build and the slightly awkward way he moved—as though he wasn't yet accustomed to his height—gave Zeke the impression he was a teenager, or in his early twenties at most. He didn't seem to be paying much attention to his surroundings, brushing by the bush where Zeke was hiding without slowing. As he passed, Zeke noticed his orange hiking boots with reflective strips on the sides.

Maybe he'd just been scouting the area. If Zeke followed him, perhaps he could get a sense of what the two were planning. He trailed behind the young man as silently as possible, keeping to the bushes, until they were almost to the river. The man smacked at his own arm several times and called out a greeting, obviously having spotted the waiting boat.

"You couldn't find them?" the one in the boat asked, his voice distorted from the face covering he wore.

"I found a cabin last night, but some guy with a shotgun came outside, so I took off. This morning, I saw him on the trail, so I checked out the cabin. Looked like women's clothes on the clothesline, but nobody was there but some old lady." He slapped his cheek. "Can't believe you dropped me off in the woods and didn't give me any mosquito repellent. Little vampires about sucked me dry."

Old lady? What was this guy talking about? Zeke would have liked to get closer, but he was afraid moving would rustle the bushes and draw their attention.

Fortunately, the man in the boat was annoyed enough to raise his voice even as the younger man drew closer. "Did you ask the old lady if she'd seen anyone?"

"She wasn't talking—just said if I didn't get out of there, she'd blast me with a shotgun. You know these bush types don't like trespassers."

"How old was this lady?"

"I don't know. She was inside the cabin, yelling through the door."

Zeke smiled to himself. *Well played, Alexis.*

"Then how do you even know she was old?" the man in the boat pointed out. "It was probably what's-her-name—the aunt."

"She sounded old."

"Yeah, well, you sound like an idiot. You need to get back up there and see if she's got the girl."

"Easy for you to say. You're not the one who might get shot, or who had to spend the night in the woods, getting eaten alive by mosquitoes." The guy slapped his other cheek. "I'm not going anywhere until I get some food and some sleep, and about a gallon of mosquito repellent." He rubbed his arm. "Besides, I think I got poison ivy."

"Poison ivy doesn't grow in Alaska."

"Well, poison something. Look." He held out his arm. "I'm getting blisters."

"Probably cow parsnip." The guy in the boat huffed. "Guess if you want something done right, ya gotta do it yourself. Fine, get in the boat. They're not going anywhere without their raft. We'll come back tomorrow and find them. But one way or another, we're not leaving tomorrow without the girl. Got it?"

"Whatever." He climbed in, and the boat took off upriver, toward Pearson Lake.

Zeke waited until he was sure they were well out of sight before coming out from the bushes. Last night's prowler seemed a bit of a bumbler, but the guy in the boat was serious, and he seemed to know more about the outdoors. They obviously weren't going to stop until they had kidnapped Keira. And they knew where she was.

Zeke could take Keira and Alexis away from the cabins to hide in the woods, which would slow the kidnappers down for a while, but it didn't solve the basic problem. If they hid from the kidnappers, they would also be hiding from rescue teams. In fact, once Keira's father had reported them missing, it might be possible for the two kidnappers to volunteer to be part of the search team. They'd been careful to cover their faces, so Keira couldn't identify them.

At least the kidnappers didn't have Keira yet, and they had a day's reprieve to figure out what to do. He headed up the trail at a run.

After the man's retreat, Alexis and Keira made no pretense of normality. Keira remained in the corner, keeping watch as best she could through the gaps in the logs. Alexis packed away the game and everything else of theirs inside the cabin, ready to move once Zeke returned. This little cabin that had been their sanctuary was no longer safe, and she had only herself to blame. But kicking herself over her decision to leave that note wasn't going to help the situation. Instead, she needed a plan.

Did they dare return to the campsite long enough to pack up the tent and other camping equipment? It was dangerous, but sleeping in the woods without proper gear wasn't exactly safe, either. What if, after they left the cabin, the kidnappers came back and tried to force Zeke to tell them where Alexis and Keira had gone? Maybe they should leave now, before he returned, so that he could honestly say he had no idea where they were. But what if the kidnapper was still there, outside, waiting for them to leave the cabin?

She wished she hadn't left her phone outside to charge. From previous river trips, she knew the whitewater sections of the river cut through bluffs and walls too steep to navigate without climbing equipment, but perhaps there was a way to circle around them and hike to Chapel Lake. The maps on her phone could give her a clue. She climbed on the bunk and peered out through the high window under the eaves toward the back of the cabin.

"What's wrong?" Keira whispered. "Did you hear something?"

"No. I was just making sure he didn't steal the phones. But they're still there."

"Maybe we should go get them," Keira suggested.

"Not yet. I promised Zeke we wouldn't leave the cabin until he returned." She didn't want to mention her fear that the kidnapper was waiting for them. "He should be back soon." Although she could have sworn well more than two hours had gone by. What if he'd tangled with the kidnappers? If he'd come to harm because of her, she'd never forgive herself.

"And then what are we going to do?" Keira was trying so hard to keep it together, but Alexis could see the fear in her eyes. And who could blame her? Alexis was terrified as well.

She went to sit down on the floor beside Keira and Poppy and reached for Keira's hand. "First of all, we should pray."

They prayed together, taking turns talking to God and asking for His protection and guidance. Alexis felt stronger. With God's help, they could do this. They'd just said their amens when Poppy let out another woof.

Keira and Alexis pressed their faces to the wall, trying to see what Poppy had heard. A moment later, familiar work boots came into view and Keira let out a sigh of relief. Alexis got up and went to the door but waited to lift the bar until Zeke knocked and called out, "It's okay. It's me."

She opened the door. He stepped inside, and she wasn't sure which of them initiated it, but suddenly, she was in his arms, snug against the strong wall of his chest, and she was holding him tight. Keira scrambled to her feet and he reached out to include her in the hug, too. "Thank God you're both all right," he murmured. "I don't know what I would have done if anything had happened to either of you."

Alexis let herself relax for a moment, secure that in that instant, she and Keira were safe. Keira seemed to feel the same, and for a long time, no one spoke. Finally, Alexis let go and stepped back. "I'm so glad you're here. It felt like you were gone forever."

"Somebody came while you were gone," Keira told him.

"I know, and that's part of the reason I took so long." Zeke explained what he'd overheard at the river.

"So, we have until tomorrow to get out of here before they return," Alexis summarized.

"Can't we just stay in the cabin with the door locked?" Keira asked. Alexis understood her reluctance to leave. This had become their safe place.

Zeke and Alexis exchanged glances. "Not if they're determined," Zeke explained gently. "We can only stock so much food and water inside the cabin. They'd just have to wait us out." Alexis was glad he hadn't mentioned other, more frightening possibilities, like setting the cabin on fire.

"Plus, we'd have to go to the bathroom eventually," Keira said, reminding them.

Zeke laughed. "Yeah, that, too."

Alexis reached for the door. "Let me get the phones and look at my maps. Maybe there's a way to hike out."

"There's not," Zeke told her as he and Keira followed her out the door. "There's a marsh between here and Pearson Lake, and the terrain on the way to Chapel Lake is too mountainous to hike without climbing gear."

"Is there any way to go cross-country to another community?"

"If you had a snowmobile or a sled-dog team in the winter, maybe," Zeke told her. "But it's probably fifty miles to the nearest village not on the Pearson River. No, the river is the highway here, either by boat in the summer or frozen over in the winter." His eyes went to the cabin under construction. "Is there any way we can build a raft from the logs in the cabin, do you think?"

Alexis was touched that he was willing to sacrifice the hard work he'd put into fitting the logs together, but she shook her head. "I've done the white water on this river. It's lower in August than in May and June, but it's still class three, and the rocks are more prominent. A log raft would never make it through in one piece—it's just not maneuverable enough. If we had a canoe, I might be able to get us through."

"I once read an article on how to build a dugout canoe," Zeke told her. "But to be big enough to carry three people, we'd need to find a tree with at least a thirty-six-inch diameter. They just don't grow that big in this area."

"And there's no way we have time to build a traditional canoe between now and tomorrow morning, even if we knew how." Alexis sighed and unplugged the phones, handing Keira's to her and opening the map on her own phone. "I think we're just going to have to get the tent and find a place to hide."

Zeke looked thoughtful. "I've only been on a few raft trips and don't know much about them, but is it possible we can repair your raft?"

"I have a patch kit and extra glue," she told him, "but I don't have nearly enough patches to cover the long slashes."

"What are raft patches made of?" Keira asked.

"Same thing as the raft, in this case Hypalon, which is a sort of synthetic rubber."

"Synthetic rubber," Zeke mused. "I think my rain jacket is basically a rubberized fabric."

"That's an idea." Alexis, who had been scrolling through the maps, considering likely places to hide, looked up. "Our fishing waders are breathable, so they probably wouldn't work, but—"

"What about the camp mats?" Keira suggested.

"Yes, another good idea." The more Alexis thought of it, the better she liked it. "And we could use the material from the thwarts to patch the main tubes, too. I hate to destroy your rain jacket, Zeke, but desperate times—"

"Don't worry about that," he told her. "How long does it take to patch a raft?"

"I've never done anything this extensive, but it takes about eight hours for the adhesive to set completely, so if I can get the patching done by tonight, we can inflate it early in the morning and see if it holds air. And while I'm working on the raft, you and Keira can be moving the camp into the woods somewhere so that we'll have a place to retreat to if it doesn't work."

"We should move everything downriver past the sandbar so that if they were to come back this afternoon, they wouldn't be able to spot the raft from their boat."

"I like that." And it would save portaging the loaded raft over the sandbar once she had patched it. "They could still hike that direction, but they would have to go looking for us."

"Okay, then." Zeke clapped his hands together. "Sounds like we have a plan."

Chapter Ten

"Here, can you hold this area flat while I apply the patch?" Alexis waited for Keira to spread her hands on either end of the slash. Alexis had intended for Keira to help Zeke move camp, but Keira had insisted on sticking with her. Alexis wasn't sure if it was because Keira felt safer in the new location past the sandbar or because she wanted to participate in putting the raft back together, but either way, an extra pair of hands was making the work go more quickly. And quick was important. The longer the glue had to set, the more likely it was to hold.

Alexis carefully brushed a thin layer of adhesive on the surface of the tube as well as on the patch she'd cut from the back of Zeke's rain jacket and smoothed it over the long cut. She pulled a roller from her pocket and ran it over the patch to make sure every inch of the dark green patch was in contact with the blue tube. It went on more smoothly than she would have expected, but they'd have to wait until tomorrow to see if it held air. Not far below it, a yellow daisy-print patch cut from their camping mat covered a Y-shaped gouge.

"This reminds me of my mom's patchwork quilts." Alexis smiled at Keira. "You know the crazy quilt on the bed in my guest room?"

"The one with all different colors of denim and fancy stitching?" Keira asked.

"That's the one. You never knew her, but your grandmother loved to quilt. Mostly she made fancy patchwork quilts in traditional patterns, but for that one, she used old jeans Dixon and I had worn out. She cut them into random pieces, sewed them together, and embroidered all the flowers and borders by hand."

"It's pretty. I think Daddy has some of her quilts in the closet, but he doesn't let me use them because he says I might ruin them."

"That's kind of the dilemma, isn't it? Keep your precious things packed away so they don't get damaged or use them and enjoy them. I'm usually in the second camp, but it's a risk." Just like taking Keira rafting had been a risk, but Alexis hadn't realized how much. She'd been prepared for bears, foul weather or the possibility of flipping the raft in the rapids, but deliberate sabotage and attempted kidnapping had never crossed her mind. She thanked God again that Zeke was there to help them. "There, that looks good. Where's the next rip?"

Poppy, who had been snoozing in the sun, suddenly raised her head. To give themselves room to work, they'd spread out the raft on a gravel beach, hidden around a bend from the junction of Serendipity Creek and the Pearson River, but still exposed if anyone should come this direction. Alexis moved between Keira and the trail, just in case, but then Poppy stood up and wagged her tail. A moment later Zeke appeared, carrying two pieces of the oar frame. "How's it going?" He set the heavy metal tubes at the edge of the beach, beside the oars and other parts and pieces he'd already brought, and reached down to pet the dog.

"Better than I expected, honestly," Alexis replied. "I think we're about halfway done."

"That's great." He picked up the water bottles they'd left resting against a tree and handed Keira and Alexis theirs before taking a drink from his own. "Still no sign of any boaters on the river. I've moved your tent and camping equipment to a spot about a quarter mile from here, up the creek to the first little falls, then left. It's in a low spot, so it's kind of buggy, but there's lots of heavy brush to hide the tent. Let's hope you won't need to use it."

"That sounds perfect." Alexis drank from her bottle and replaced the lid.

"Good. I'll go after the rest of the frame and make sure I didn't leave anything behind." He set his bottle on the ground and ran off down the trail. Despite having moved a massive amount of equipment, his gait hadn't slowed all day.

Alexis pressed her hands to her lower back, sore from bending over the tubes all afternoon. Keira came and casually wrapped her arms around Alexis's waist, the way she used to do when she was just a little girl. Alexis draped an arm over Keira's shoulders. Together, they watched Zeke disappear into the trees. "Do you think he'll be okay here, after we're gone?" Keira asked.

"I think so," Alexis answered her. "Once we're out of the picture, the bad guys have no reason to bother Zeke."

"I don't mean that. I mean, he'll be all by himself. Won't he get lonely?"

Alexis had wondered the same thing, but it wasn't any of their business. "I don't know, Keira. This is the life he chose."

"But why? It's not that he doesn't like people. He's been so nice to us."

"Yes, he has. I don't know why Zeke wants or needs to live alone out here, but I'm sure he has his reasons." Alexis gave Keira's shoulders a squeeze. "Guess we'd better get back to work. We've still got plenty of patches to apply."

They worked steadily for the rest of the afternoon. Once Zeke had finished breaking down their camp, he'd hurried along the raft repair by cutting and preparing patches so that as soon as Keira and Alexis finished applying one, the next patch was ready. Finally, in the early evening, Alexis finished the last patch. "There. I want to go over the tubes one more time to make sure we didn't miss anything, but I think we're done."

Zeke examined the patches. "You did an amazing job applying these without leaving any loose edges."

"It's kind of a Frankenboat," Alexis said. "But if the patches hold air, it should get us through the rapids to Chapel Lake. We need to let them cure for eight hours before we pump up the tubes, so tomorrow morning will be the test."

"Okay, then. Once you've done your last check, let's head back to the cabin. There should be enough daylight left to charge your phones, and we might as well eat up that salmon we've been smoking."

"I thought you were going to save that for winter," Alexis said.

"I changed my mind."

"Are we spending the night in the tent?" Keira asked.

Alexis and Zeke looked at each other. "They said they weren't coming back until tomorrow," Zeke reminded her.

Would they be safer in a tent, hidden from the kidnappers? Alexis's head said yes, but her heart was leading her back to the sturdy little cabin that had kept them safe thus far. "I'm leaning toward the cabin."

"Me, too," Keira agreed, and Zeke nodded.

"That's settled, then." Alexis walked around to the

other side of the raft, where she'd applied the first patches. "Here. Let's do one final check for nicks and holes I might have missed."

Zeke nodded. "Then I'll show you how to find your tent and other gear on the way back."

All three of them inspected every inch of the raft, and they agreed every cut and tear had been covered and all the patches appeared to be holding. Ordinarily, Alexis would have clamped the patches to the tubes while they set, but they didn't have that many clamps, so she was just going to have to trust that the glue would hold. They threw a tarp over the raft and covered it with leaves and branches to make it harder to spot. The other equipment went into the woods, hidden from view. Finally, satisfied that this was the best they could do for tonight, Alexis reached for Keira with one hand and Zeke with the other. "Let's go home."

That evening, the three of them went through the routines they'd established over the past few days, building fires, preparing dinner, washing up. But all the time they worked, Alexis kept glancing around, startling every time the wind rustled the leaves or a bird called. After dinner, while Zeke and Keira toasted the marshmallows Zeke had come across while moving camp, Alexis walked a few steps away from the light of the fire and stared into the woods. What if she'd made the wrong decision, and the kidnappers came back tonight? But Zeke was here, and that made her feel safer. It wasn't fair to lay all this on Zeke's broad shoulders, but he'd stepped up as their protector and she was so glad he did.

Tomorrow was another story. Once they'd pumped up the raft and hit the river, she and Keira would be on their own once again. What if the raft wouldn't hold air? What if she couldn't get them through the rapids? What if the kidnappers—

Zeke touched her shoulder. "You okay?"

"I guess so." She turned to face him and managed a smile. "Just wrestling with some doubts."

He nodded slowly. "I know all about those. Haven't found them to be particularly helpful, though."

"Oh, yeah? What do you suggest I do about it?"

"I don't have answers." He looked up at the sky, just beginning to turn pink as the sun dipped lower. "Maybe you should talk to someone who does."

She followed his gaze toward the heavens. "You're right. Keep an eye on Keira for me for a few minutes, would you?"

"Sure." He turned. "Hey, Keira. You got another one of those marshmallows for me? I dropped the last one in the fire."

Alexis walked to the back of the cabin, where she could get an unobstructed view of the sunset. On the edges of the woods, beside the creek, pink fireweed bloomed. Poppy followed along and sat on her foot, leaning against her leg. Alexis smiled and rested a hand on Poppy's head, touched at the dog's loyalty, considering she could be missing out on a dropped marshmallow back at the fire.

Alexis watched as the sun began to paint the wispy clouds floating overhead the same shade as the fireweed. The pink intensified, spreading from the clouds to the snowcapped peaks of Denali and Foraker and on to paint the entire western sky crimson. God had created it all, the mountains, the sun, the trees, the flowers. A God who could do all this could surely keep an eye on Keira and her. *Are not two sparrows sold for a penny? And not one of them will fall to the ground apart from your Father's care.*

She prayed then, with her eyes wide open to receive this gift. Some of the prayer she spoke aloud, some just in her thoughts and some was simply sharing her feelings, but she gave over her doubts and her fears and she thanked the Lord for all He had done to protect them, most of all for sending them to Zeke. She prayed that despite whatever it was that had driven Zeke to this life, he would find peace and healing.

In the distance, an eagle soared, silhouetted against the darkening sky. He glided effortlessly, floating over all the turmoil and fear below, and Alexis felt her fears and doubts begin to float away as well. They would be back for sure, but for this moment, she felt light, peaceful. God was good.

Zeke buttoned his jacket. The sun hadn't risen high enough to reach over the trees into the clearing yet this morning. The three of them had been up and eating breakfast at sunrise, which came at five thirty, according to Keira's phone. While Alexis and Keira gathered up their things to carry to the boat, Zeke handled a few last-minute chores as well. He fed his sourdough starter, filled water bottles, doused the fires, and made sure his tools were put away safe and out of the elements.

Today looked like a clear, sunny day, but the weather could turn quickly. After packing a few things in his own backpack, he shrugged it onto his shoulders and strapped his rifle to the outside. Then he went to see if Alexis and Keira were ready to go. They needed to get the raft pumped up and moved down the river before the two men he'd seen yesterday made their way downstream from Pearson Lake.

He picked up the two heaviest-looking bags they had gathered. Most of the bigger things he'd already taken down to the hidden campsite with the tent. Alexis and Keira gathered up the other bits and pieces. Alexis met his eyes, took a deep breath and nodded. It was time.

"Ready?" he asked Keira.

"Sure." Keira gave her shoulders a shake to settle her pack and picked up the dry bag containing freeze-dried meals.

"Let's cross the creek here and angle down to the river on the other side." Just in case the would-be kidnappers were early birds, Zeke didn't want to run into them on the trail. He led the way across the stepping-stone path to the other side of the creek, and then through the woods, glad he'd memorized all the game trails in the area. When they arrived at the beach, the raft equipment and tubes appeared undisturbed, the leaves and branches they'd used to cover them still in place. The sun shone on the beach, and they all shucked their jackets before carefully uncovering the raft.

"So far, so good," Alexis said. "I don't see any patches curling away."

Zeke retrieved the pump from where he'd stowed it out of sight. "How does this work?"

"We hook it up here." Alexis wiped the end of the hose from the pump with her shirttail, unscrewed a cap covering the port on the raft and set the hose in place, giving it a twist to snap the connection together. "Now comes the hard work."

"Let me." Zeke positioned his feet on the fins at the bottom of the pump, raised the handle and pushed it down, forcing a whoosh of air into the tube.

"That's one." Alexis grinned. "Now we just need to do that about three thousand more times, and we're done."

"Guess I'd better get busy, then." Zeke continued to pump, steadily. Meanwhile, Alexis and Keira reassembled the oar frame and prepared all the equipment to go into the raft. They would wait to move the camping gear until they had some idea whether the unconventional patches would hold air.

He'd been pumping for about ten minutes and the

left side of the raft had gone from pancake flat to mounding when Alexis handed him a water bottle. "My turn."

"I'm fine," he assured her, although he was breathing hard.

She chuckled. "Pace yourself. We have two more chambers to inflate after this." She set her feet and started pumping.

Zeke went to stand beside Keira while he drank deeply. Watching Alexis work the pump, he realized this would be a regular part of a fly-in raft trip. "You two have already done this once, when the floatplane dropped you off at Pearson Lake, right?" he asked Keira.

Keira nodded. "Alexis let me pump some, but she did most of it."

Impressive. "How long did it take?"

"Forever," Keira sighed, but then admitted, "About an hour."

"But that was with breaks," Alexis interjected between pants. "I think we can do it in thirty minutes if we take turns."

Zeke looked at the position of the sun. About two hours had elapsed from daybreak until now. It took about an hour for a motorboat to make its way from Pearson Lake to the mouth of Serendipity Creek, and another hour for the men to reach the cabin. If the two men had left at the crack of dawn, they would be discovering empty cabins right about now. Although Zeke had made a point of putting out the fires and protecting his tools, he'd purposely left a shirt on the clothesline and the coffeepot sitting beside the fire ring to make the place look as occupied as possible. If the men were good trackers, they might be able to pick up their trail and follow them to the beach, but an experienced outdoorsman wouldn't have brushed against cow parsnip.

Still, the older guy had known about the plant, and if he noticed the raft gone, he might guess the direction they would take. They needed to get this raft inflated and moving downriver as soon as possible. He took one more drink and stepped forward. "Tagging in."

"All yours." Alexis stepped aside and let him pump. As the tube filled with air, she bent down to push against the tubes and test the pressure. "Stop pumping for just a sec." She held her ear near the tube. After listening for a moment, she smiled. "I don't hear any leaks. That's good news. Let's start on chamber number two and see if it holds. I wouldn't want to take a partial raft through white water, but if we can get two out of three holding air, we can at least float down a little farther."

She removed the hose from the port, moved the pump to the other side of the raft and clicked it in place to fill up the next chamber with air. While Zeke continued pumping, she replaced the first cap and checked all the patches once again.

They continued to pump, taking turns, and in a little over twenty minutes from when they'd started,

Alexis announced that chamber number three seemed to be holding air as well. She and Keira exchanged high fives. "All right, then. We need to get the rest of these tubes pumped up tight, but in the meantime, we can bring down all the camping equipment." She looked the raft over. "Just to reduce weight and keep us floating higher, I think I'll leave the Dutch oven, camp chairs and one of the ice chests behind. Okay?"

"That's fine," Zeke answered. "Do you want me pumping or bringing your camping gear?"

"Gear, please. I'll get these tubes topped up and strap in the oar frame."

With Keira's help, Zeke was able to gather up all the camping gear and get it to the boat in one trip. By that time, Alexis had managed to pump the raft up tight. He helped her lift the heavy oar frame into place, and she tightened the straps that held it to the raft. "Let's shove this closer to the water before we load," she suggested.

Together the three of them pushed the patchwork raft to the edge. When they stopped, Zeke thought he heard something above the usual sounds of nature. He held up a finger. "Listen." They all froze. For a long moment, the only sound was the water rushing by, but with another breath of wind, he caught it again—the sound of a motor.

"They're here," Alexis whispered. "We need to go. Fast."

Immediately, the three of them threw the camping gear and equipment into the raft. Alexis tossed a life jacket to Keira and motioned for her to climb to the front of the raft while she locked the oars in place. Poppy hopped in after her. Alexis turned to Zeke while she buckled her life jacket. "I can't thank you enough—"

"Thank me later." He positioned his hands against the back of the raft, ready to push them into the water as soon as Alexis was in position. "I'll jump in as soon as you're in the water."

Alexis's eyes opened wide. "You're coming with us?"

"I am." He couldn't desert them now. Once the kidnappers figured out they were gone, they could very well get a raft of their own and follow. Even if they didn't, there was the danger of taking a damaged raft through the white water. Zeke was no rafting expert, but he wasn't going to let them face it alone. "Is that okay?"

Alexis looked at him and blinked. For a split second he was afraid she might be about to cry, but instead her face broke into a wide smile. "It's okay." She pointed. "Grab that spare life vest."

"Are we going or what?" Keira demanded, unable to hear what they were saying.

Alexis climbed into the oaring seat. "We're going," she told Keira. "All three of us."

Chapter Eleven

Zeke pushed them into the current and jumped onto the raft. Alexis waited until she was sure he was settled, and then oared the raft into the middle of the river, where the current was strongest, confident that the bend of the river would shield them from the men in the motorboat. The breeze picked up a little, and now they could plainly hear the engine noise, and then the sudden quiet that must have meant the men had docked.

Even though the current carried the raft along at a good clip, Alexis continued to row, still facing upstream, where she could keep an eye on the river behind them. If the men in the boat had noticed that the vandalized raft was missing from the shoreline, and surely they would have, it probably wouldn't take them long to start searching for Keira and Alexis somewhere along this river, and Alexis wanted to be as far away as possible before that happened.

The raft handling was a little wonky, but considering all the patches and the fact that they'd dumped in the gear without any attempt to balance the load, that wasn't surprising. What was surprising was the man sitting on the ice chest in the back of her raft, looking right at home.

He caught her eye as she rowed and flashed her a grin. She smiled back. She could hardly believe this was the same man who had looked so annoyed when they stumbled onto his property just days ago. They were not his responsibility, but almost from the start, he'd taken them in. He'd done everything to keep them safe, and now he was leaving his home behind to go with them, to protect them. He had to know, after seeing the damage to the raft, that the kidnappers might very well take out their frustration on his cabins. He had every reason to stay behind. And yet here he was.

Once they'd made it around two more river bends, she rested the oars on the tubes and turned around to check on Keira. Since they'd had to use the thwarts where Keira would normally sit for patch material, Keira was sprawled on the floor, leaning back against the tube, with an arm around Poppy. When she saw Alexis looking, she smiled and gave her a thumbs-up. Alexis chuckled, and Poppy wagged her tail.

They came to another junction where a creek, this one much bigger than Serendipity Creek, spilled into the Pearson. The river widened, and the current sped up a notch. The river got trickier here, too, with scattered boulders and some dicey holes. Pushing one oar forward and the other back, Alexis spun the raft so that she was facing downstream, where she could better watch for obstacles, and let the river carry them forward. Zeke pointed at the shoreline, and she glanced over to see a moose calf skipping along the bank, his mother keeping a close eye from her spot at the edge of the woods. Keira pulled her phone from her pocket and snapped a picture. One of those special little Alaska moments that almost made this feel like an ordinary float trip. Almost.

If Alexis recalled correctly, the first white water would come up in about five miles. It wasn't the most technical part of the trip, but it would be a test to see if their patchwork raft could make it through. She kept an eye out for a good landing spot, and about twenty minutes later, she saw one, a nice gentle grassy slope on the inside curve of the river. She leaned on the oars and hauled them to the edge, bumping the front edge of the raft onto the grass.

"Taking a break?" Zeke asked.

"We need to lash everything down," Alexis explained. "We'll be coming up on the first rapids before long."

Keira grabbed the bowline and vaulted over the raft tube onto the ground, then looked around for something to tie up to. Alexis pointed at a big rock. "That would work."

Keira looped the rope around the rock and then

turned upriver and lifted a hand to shade her eyes. "Do you think they're still coming?"

"I don't," Alexis answered. "That sandbar by Serendipity Creek has built up higher than when I used to float this river. If we hadn't reassembled downriver, we would have had to unload the raft and portage it over. An aluminum riverboat with a jet motor weighs at least a thousand pounds. And even if they could get it over that sandbar, there's no way they could make it through the rocks we've been dodging for the last few miles."

Alexis folded the oars and got out of the raft. The tubes felt a little spongy, but not bad.

"So we're safe?" Keira persisted.

Before Alexis could reassure her, Poppy jumped out of the raft and began sniffing the grass along the shoreline, her tail wagging. Zeke chuckled. "Your dog seems to think so."

"And I agree with Poppy."

"Are we camping here, then?" Keira asked.

"No. We've still got plenty of daylight left and I want to get some more river miles before we stop. If we can get through the first set of rapids today, we can run the second set and make it to Chapel Lake tomorrow, when our floatplane was originally scheduled to pick us up. Right now, I just want to rearrange the load, pump up the tubes and lash everything down."

Zeke pushed on the tube. "It does seem a little softer."

"That's not surprising, but it's doing well enough to get us through." She dug out the pump, attached it to the first port and started to pump, but Zeke waved her away.

"Let me. I don't know how to arrange the gear, but I can do this."

"Thanks." She couldn't say how much his quiet support meant. She wasn't sure that if she were alone with Keira, she would be holding it together nearly this well. Just by being there in the back of the raft, he had made her feel protected and cared for. She could tell by the way Keira stood near him now that she felt the same.

Alexis went to work, unloading most of the gear and repacking it inside a large mesh bag that she could strap onto the D rings on the tubes. While Zeke moved the pump to the next chamber, she set the gear bag in the front of the raft, lashed the dry bags to the sides, and dug out Poppy's life jacket and the white-water helmets. That was when she realized she'd only brought two. Shoot. She always brought an extra life jacket in case one got damaged or misplaced, but it had never occurred to her that she might need a spare helmet for another passenger.

Zeke finished pumping up the third chamber. "How does this feel?"

Alexis pushed on the tube. "Perfect." She handed out water bottles and energy bars. "Here, let's fuel up."

"Ooh, chocolate and almond." Keira tore the wrapper and bit into her bar. "This will be my first real white water," she told Zeke as she chewed. "Daddy wouldn't let me go until I turned twelve."

"I've only been down this way once before," Zeke told her. "It's a thrill."

"Alexis will get us through," Keira assured him. "She's the best."

Zeke looked at Alexis with a little smile on his face. At first, she thought he was amused, but then she realized his expression was more like admiration. "You're right. She is the best."

Since Zeke had admitted he knew little about rafts, his endorsement shouldn't mean much, but it did. It was good that he and Keira had confidence in her ability to shepherd them through the white water. She planned to do everything in her power to live up to it. "Here." She tossed the helmets their way. "Put these on."

Keira buckled hers on immediately. Zeke started to follow suit, but then he frowned. "Where's yours?"

"I only brought two."

"Then you wear this one."

Alexis shook her head. "I'm secure in the oarsman seat. If something goes wrong, you're much more likely to fall out than I am. Not that anything will go wrong," she emphasized, for Keira's sake. "This is only class two. I've run it at least a dozen times, and I've never flipped a raft."

"Then I don't have to worry," Zeke told her as he deliberately returned the helmet. "I trust you."

He obviously wasn't backing down, and they didn't

have time to waste. She accepted the helmet and put it on. She would just need to be extra careful to get them through upright. She untied the bowline. "All right, then. Let's go."

Once Keira, Poppy and Alexis were in the raft, Zeke pushed them off and scrambled in. Alexis oared them into the current. The raft seemed to be handling better, although it still had a bit of a starboard tug. She positioned the raft at an angle and looked forward until she spotted the first rapids. "Okay, you two. Get down lower in the boat. I want to come out the other side with the same number of passengers." She looked over her shoulder to check on Keira. "You all right?"

"I'm good." Keira knelt down on the floor where she could still see over the tubes, her eyes wide.

This and the other rapid just before Chapel Lake were supposed to be the highlights of the trip, not a necessary obstacle in their escape from kidnappers. Were the two men still back there, coming for them? She'd told Keira the truth that the powerboat couldn't go any farther, but that didn't rule out the possibility of the kidnappers bringing a raft of their own to chase after them. Or worse, kayaks, which would move much faster than the raft. But they wouldn't be able to take Keira away on a kayak, so Alexis could probably rule out that possibility, at least. Anyway, one problem at a time, and the immediate goal was to get the raft safely through the rapids.

Zeke settled on the floor of the raft. It looked a

little cramped, but Alexis felt a lot safer with him there than perched on the ice chest. He gave her a reassuring smile. "All set."

They were ready. Now it was up to her. "Guide me, Lord." The familiar prayer left her lips just as she spotted the first hole, on the right side of the river. She swung left and took them over a shallow drop with a splash that caught Zeke by surprise, judging by his sudden whoop. Keira laughed, just in time to take a face full of the same wave. Then it was Zeke's turn to laugh.

Alexis ferried the raft toward the left bank to avoid a sleeper, a boulder lurking just below the surface, and then spun off around another rock the size of a baby elephant so as to miss the souse hole on the left. After a series of riffles, the water quieted for a short stretch before dropping them into a boulder garden, which required constant shifts for Alexis to pick her way around and between the rocks. She loved this part of rafting, the thrill of maneuvering the boat as they almost flew down the river, caught in the current and riding it along.

Even with all the patches, the raft felt nimble now, scooting here and there at the touch of an oar. The river took a bend and there was a ledge she remembered with a backroller at the bottom. No way around it, so they'd have to go through. She squared up the raft, gave a push with the oars and grinned. "Hang on and be ready if I call high side."

"What's that?" Keira called.

Before she could explain, in they went with a huge splash, the raft bucking like a rodeo horse. The wave brought the left tube up. "High side," Alexis shouted. "Lean left!"

Both Keira and Zeke jumped into action, throwing themselves toward the left side of the raft and weighing it down long enough to keep the raft upright until they shot on past the roller. Three more drops, and they were through the rapid and floating peacefully along, still right side up and all in the boat. A success. Alexis uttered a silent prayer of thanks and turned to Keira, who had settled back onto the floor of the raft.

"Good job back there. What did you think of your first rapid?"

Keira grinned. "Awesome!"

In the back of the raft, Zeke chuckled. "I concur."

The river was picking up speed, and Alexis recognized the bluffs far up ahead as the start of the biggest rapid. As she recalled, there was a good camp spot just upstream of the rapids along a dry wash. Hopefully, she remembered correctly, because one way or the other, they needed to stop. They rounded a bend, and she spotted a shallow gravel slope punctuated by a dozen or so school bus–sized boulders that some glacier carried there and left behind in the last ice age. They should be able to set up the tent behind the rocks and it wouldn't be visible from the river. She oared the raft up to the shore.

Keira looked at the sky. "It's not that late. We could go farther."

Alexis shook her head. "No, the second set of rapids is just up ahead, and they're more technical than the ones we passed earlier. I'll need to scout them before we run them. Besides, shadows from the bluffs make it hard to read the river in the evening. We can run them in the morning and make it to Chapel Lake by noon. The floatplane is due to meet us at three." She winked at Keira. "Besides, I'm sure you'll want to charge your phone so you can take pictures to share with your friends once you're back to city life."

"Good idea. Where did you put the charger?"

"We'll find it. Let's set up camp first."

Once they'd unloaded what they needed and pitched the tent behind the rocks, they pushed the raft ashore at the edge of the beach next to a thick grove of alders. Without being asked, Zeke went to work, cutting branches and shielding the raft from casual view. Keira helped him, while Alexis arranged their sleeping bags in the tent and built a small fire ring behind the biggest boulders, where the light wouldn't be visible from the other side. Not that anyone should be rafting down the river in the dark, but it didn't hurt to take precautions.

She gestured toward the wash. "I'm going to climb up and head over to the bluffs to scout the river while we've still got some light."

"We'll cook," Zeke offered. "Right, Keira?"

"As soon as we set up the phone charger," she agreed.

Zeke chuckled. "I see you have your priorities."

Alexis scrambled up the scree pile and followed a ridge to the top, where she could make her way to the bluffs overlooking the rapids. Good thing she did, because at some point, a huge cottonwood had fallen halfway across the river, just past a technically challenging rock garden that would have made it difficult to see in time. There was a reason they called fallen trees like that sweepers—they could sweep you right off your raft. It would be a tricky maneuver, but now that she knew it was there, she could handle it. Once she was satisfied with her plan on how to navigate the rapids in the morning, she returned to camp.

Zeke waved when he saw her coming. They'd left behind most of the heavier foods, grates and cooking pots, but Zeke had found some chicken breasts at the bottom of the ice chest and was roasting them on a spit he'd rigged up over the fire. When the scent from the chicken reached her, her stomach growled. The energy bar and apple she'd eaten for lunch were a distant memory. Keira was digging out packages of freeze-dried mac and cheese and some carrots. After a day of oaring, a gourmet feast couldn't have tasted better.

After the day they'd had, it was no surprise that Keira was yawning even before the sun had set. Alexis was exhausted as well. "What do you say we turn in and get an early start?" She unzipped the tent, allowed Keira to crawl inside and followed her. "Zeke, are you coming?"

He shook his head. "It's warm out. I'll sleep out under the stars tonight."

Alexis suspected it wasn't a sudden yearning for stargazing that had Zeke choosing to stay outside. That protective instinct of his wouldn't let him relax when there was any possibility of danger from the river. And she knew it would be futile to try to talk him out of it. Funny that after only knowing him for a few days, she could read him so well. She smiled. "Okay, but feel free to come inside if the bugs get too bad."

"There's a little breeze. I'll be fine."

Alexis and Keira snuggled into their bags and Alexis let her eyes drift shut. She could rest easy, knowing Zeke was out there. She silently gave thanks to God, for watching over them as they escaped, for keeping them safe through the rapids and, most of all, for Zeke.

Chapter Twelve

Zeke added another piece of wood to the fire and settled down beside it, leaning against the rock face that separated the camp from the river. He listened but heard only the normal river sounds. It was finally fully dark. No one would be boating now. They were safe, at least until dawn. He should get some sleep, but his eyes refused to close.

He heard a sudden noise from inside the tent, a gasp. Instantly, he was alert, ready to leap into action, but the noise was followed by the whir of the zipper on the bug screen opening. Alexis crawled outside. "Oh, good. You're awake."

"You okay?" he asked.

"Fine. Just a silly dream. Something about jet boats. Must have watched too many adventure movies." She zipped the tent closed behind her. "You're not sleeping?"

"Dozed a bit. I told you, I don't sleep much." He

scooted over to expose more of the dry bag he was sitting on. "Pull up a chair."

She sank down beside him. "I've heard some of the greatest minds in the world got by on hardly any sleep, like Thomas Edison and Leonardo da Vinci. I wonder if it's genetic?"

"Not in my case. I used to sleep eight hours like clockwork."

"What happened?"

He mumbled a nonanswer. She had enough to worry about without adding his baggage. Before she could repeat the question, he asked, "When you climbed the bluff, did you see anything that concerned you?"

She hesitated as though debating whether to let him change the subject before she replied. "You mean coming up the river behind us, or in the rapids themselves?"

"Either, I guess."

"From what I can tell, we're the only boat on the river right now, so that's good news. As far as the rapids, there's a big sweeper downriver a way, but now that I know about it, I can handle it."

He nodded. "After watching you today, I get the feeling you can handle just about anything this river might throw at you."

"I've run this river many times. Not in recent years, but I would do it two or three times a summer when I was guiding for my dad, and so far, I've never flipped a raft. Let's hope my record holds."

He was confident it would. She'd been almost unnaturally calm running through the rapids, as though she had some secret knowledge. He picked up a small stone, polished smooth from tumbling in the river, and rubbed it between his finger and thumb. "Today, just before you went into the rapids, you said something."

She nodded. "Just a little prayer. Whenever I'm about to go into rapids, I always ask God to guide me."

"And does He?" Zeke was genuinely curious.

"I believe He does. More than once, I've been about to go one way and then I feel like I should reflect and go the other way instead."

He'd felt like that at times in his life. Most recently just before taking off on that final flight. If only he'd paid attention. He tossed the stone from one hand to the other. "I'm fascinated by the way you talk to God so easily, like a friend. It reminds me of someone I used to know."

"Who's that?"

He set the stone down. This wasn't Alexis's burden. But he couldn't seem to shake the need to talk about it. "Her name was Dani."

"Was?"

"She's gone now." Zeke stared into the fire, but he was seeing Dani's face, smiling at him. Always smiling, even when she was in pain. Even when she must have known she was dying.

"You loved her," Alexis whispered.

"I did." And then he spoke the words that would forever change the relationship between them, but Alexis should know what kind of a person he was. "And I killed her."

He waited for the horror he knew he would see in her eyes. For her to pull away, to retreat. But neither of those things happened. Instead, she asked softly, "Do you want to tell me about it?"

Did he? "It's a long story."

She touched his arm. "We've got all night."

That was true. He knew he wouldn't sleep any more this evening, and he doubted Alexis would, either. "I don't know where to start."

She leaned forward so that she could meet his eyes. "Why don't you start at the beginning?"

"The beginning," he murmured. For a long moment, he looked down, gathering his thoughts. "I guess that would be when I came to Alaska, a little over six years ago. My mom had just died, and since I didn't have any other close family, I thought I'd try someplace different. A fresh start."

"And was it? A fresh start?"

He nodded. "Alaska was good for me. I worked with a great group of people. One of the guys in my group took me up in his small plane, and I was hooked. I had some money from a life insurance policy my mom had through her job, so I decided to take flying lessons."

"How did that go?"

"Lessons went well. For me, flying seemed to

come as naturally as walking. I got in my hours, got my license and kept flying. Two years ago, three of us in the physical therapy practice where I worked went in together and bought a used Piper PA-18 Super Cub with floats that we shared." He paused, remembering. "Thanksgiving of that year, one of the senior partners invited those of us without local family to dinner, and he introduced me to his niece, Danielle."

Alexis smiled. "Was it love at first sight?"

"Not exactly." He smiled, remembering. "I figured she was out of my league. But then Mark, the senior partner, made us do that thing where we went around the table saying what we were thankful for. I mentioned the plane, and when it was Dani's turn, she said she was thankful I was going to take her up in my plane. Which was news to me."

Alexis smiled. "So did you take her up?"

"I did. The very next day."

"Tell me about Dani. What was she like?"

"Well, she was a nurse. She worked in the maternity ward. She especially loved working with the tiny premature babies."

"That must take a lot of patience."

"She could be patient, but it didn't always come naturally." He laughed. "Once, for instance, she didn't like a certain doctor's brusque attitude toward one of the mothers with a baby in ICU. According to one of the other nurses she worked with, by the time Dani was through with him, that doctor was almost begging for mercy."

Alexis chuckled. "Sounds like he deserved it."

"I'm sure he did. But she told me later that she shouldn't have let her temper get away from her. She used to pray for patience sometimes, and then laugh because her prayer wasn't answered fast enough."

"So, she had a sense of humor."

"Definitely. Anyway, long story short, last summer, I asked her to marry me. She said yes." He stared into the flame, remembering how she'd loved the ring. The plans they'd made together. Until... "We celebrated by flying to a remote lodge up toward Nikolai for Labor Day weekend. It was beautiful there. But on Sunday night, the weather turned, and on Monday, the ceiling was too low to fly. Which was inconvenient because I had agreed to play golf Tuesday evening with some friends. But the weather report called for a window around three Monday afternoon, and the clouds lifted briefly. Dani didn't want to risk it, but—" He blew out a long breath, remembering that feeling telling him not to fly, and the way he'd dismissed it. "Do you know in the Bible where Satan takes Jesus to the top of the temple and dares him to throw himself down?"

"And Jesus says, 'You shall not put the Lord Your God to the test,'" she quoted.

"Exactly. But I did. I thought I was such a hotshot pilot that I could handle anything. Pure arrogance. And for a golf game, no less." He shook his head.

"Once the clouds lifted enough to take off, we did. And we made it fine until we reached Rainy Pass." He looked up at the stars without seeing them. "The clouds were so thick, I couldn't even tell up from down. I thought I was still on course…until I saw the mountain rushing at us. Then it was too late."

"What happened?"

"We crash-landed on the mountainside. Dani was badly hurt, but still alive. I'd activated the emergency beacon, but the same weather I should have taken seriously kept the rescue helicopter grounded for two more days. By the time they made it, she was gone. And it was all because of my arrogance."

"I'm so sorry." She reached for his hand, and he let her take it even though he didn't deserve comfort. "Were you hurt?"

"I was, broke several bones, needed some surgery. I was still in the hospital when they had her memorial service, so at least I didn't have to face her family. I can't imagine how hard it would have been for them to have me there, knowing I was the reason she was dead."

"You think they blamed you?"

"How could they not? I blame me. It was my fault that she died. She was such a good person." He took a breath and let it out. "Her last words before she lost consciousness were that she loved me and forgave me. She should have been the one to live, not me." She was innocent. He was the one who had tested the Lord.

Alexis tilted her head in that way she did when she was thinking things over. "I don't profess to understand these things, but I do know God is willing to forgive much worse sins than a lapse in judgment. Even when it leads to tragedy. You're human, like the rest of us."

He shrugged. Easy to say, but he knew better.

She squeezed his hand. "You know, it sounds like you have lots of good memories with Dani. Don't let the bad ones chase away the good."

He didn't answer. How could she see anything good in this? He'd accidentally killed a wonderful human being. There was no redemption there.

After a moment, Alexis asked, "How did you wind up building a cabin in the wilderness?"

He sighed. "It took me a while to recover from my injuries and build up my strength, but I found even after I was physically healed, I couldn't do my job. I couldn't make the decisions I needed to make for my clients' therapy, because I had no confidence that they were the right decisions. I tried praying, but I didn't feel like I could talk to God, that He heard me, much less answered me. I tore up my pilot's license and quit my job. Then I saw a property for sale, where I could be alone and not have to be responsible for anyone except myself. I thought maybe I'd find God out here."

"And did you?" she asked.

Not really. "I found gratitude in the logs He provided, and some satisfaction in fitting them together, but I can't say that God and I are exactly communicating."

"I wonder—" she began, but stopped.

"Wonder what?"

"I was just thinking—do you remember the story of Jonah?"

"The prophet who was swallowed by a big fish?"

"Exactly. Jonah was called to go one place, and instead he ran away. God had to send a fish to bring him back. Do you think God called you to the wilderness? Or could it be that you ran to the wilderness to hide from God?"

A good question. "I don't know. Like I said, we're not really on speaking terms these days."

"Or maybe God is speaking and you're just not hearing. I have to wonder if you're mistakenly trying to earn your way back into God's good graces by sacrificing your job and your relationships, but it's not necessary. You've confessed your mistake and sincerely repented. Jesus has already made the ultimate sacrifice for you."

Could she be right? He got up and paced a few steps before turning back. "You think I was wrong to build my cabin and live alone out here?"

"Well, I can hardly say that, since if it wasn't for you being in that place, Keira and I might very well be kidnapped. Or worse." She caught his gaze and held it. "I understand why you feel the way you do, but if you're going to beat yourself up about your mistake, then you have to give yourself credit for what you've done for Keira and me. You've gone above and beyond to help us."

"It doesn't excuse my past."

"Your past isn't what's most important." She moved to stand in front of him. "When I look at you," she said, reaching up to cup her hand over his cheek, "I see the face of a hero."

"I don't think so." How could she believe in him when she knew what he'd done?

She didn't waver. "I know what I see."

Could it be true? After the terrible thing he'd done, could he still be a hero for Alexis? Something flickered in his peripheral vision and he looked up. A swirling ribbon of green ran across the sky.

"The first northern lights of the season," Alexis whispered in awe.

He stared as the beautiful lights shimmered and swirled in the sky, and then his gaze dropped to Alexis's face, no less beautiful. His eyes sought hers, looking for doubts, for recriminations, but her clear gaze met his, tender and loving. He moved his face closer to hers and she tilted her chin, ready to receive his kiss. Tentatively, he touched her lips with his. Her arms went around his neck, pulling him closer, and he kissed her again, less tentatively.

And there, kissing this incredible woman under the northern lights, something heavy and painful inside of him loosened and fell away, leaving him feeling like he could almost float up into the sky and dance among the lights. There was an unfamiliar sensation in his heart, something he hadn't felt in a very long time.

Peace.

Chapter Thirteen

Early the next morning, they finished breakfast, pumped up the tubes, and packed up the raft in record time. Zeke waited for the others to settle in. Keira took her place up front, and Alexis climbed into the oaring seat, her dark hair tied back with a bright pink bandanna. Zeke smiled to himself. That bandanna was so Alexis: practical, but with a certain flair.

"Let's go, Poppy," she called.

The dog came running from the woods and jumped into the raft, taking her place beside Keira. Zeke gave the old dog a moment and then shoved them off the shore and jumped into the raft.

No one had come down the river after them last night, but that didn't mean they were out of danger. Zeke didn't know much about rafting, but he knew class three rapids were nothing to sneeze at, even with a raft in good condition, much less one held together by patches and hope. But this was Alexis's area of expertise. She had assessed the rapids and the tree that had fallen across the river as something she could handle. All Zeke could do was hold on. And pray.

Maybe Alexis was right. Maybe the reason he didn't feel like God heard his prayers was because Zeke hadn't been listening. He had never asked God for forgiveness for what he'd done, because he didn't feel like he deserved it. But maybe that was the point of forgiveness. If Alexis could see him as a hero, even after she knew the truth about him, then maybe—just maybe—he was worth forgiving.

The roar grew louder as they approached the rough water. "Keira, put the phone away and hunker down," Alexis called. Keira, who had been snapping photos, complied, tucking the phone into her pocket and zipping it closed. Poppy, veteran rafter that she was, braced herself and lifted her head to sniff the air as they entered the rapids.

He saw the prayer for guidance on Alexis's lips and added his own. Several boulders studded the rushing water. They were headed straight toward one the size of a compact car. With the flick of an oar, Alexis sent the raft spinning so that it circled around the boulder instead of crashing into it. She dipped and dodged their way between rocks and called out a warning to "Hold on," just before they dropped over a ledge with a splash that provoked a squeal from Keira. Once they were past the spot, Poppy gave a hard shake, spraying Keira with water once again. Zeke chuckled.

They rounded a bend, and Zeke spotted another ledge coming up. This one had an unexpected hazard. A big blond grizzly had stationed himself at the base on one side, ready to snag any salmon foolish enough to make the leap to the next level of the river. Keira's eyes went wide. Zeke called a warning to Alexis, who nodded to show she'd spotted the bear as well. With a quick flick of the oars, she spun around and to the other side, giving the bear a wide berth.

Up ahead, the water on the right side of the river churned in a whirlpool. On the left, a set of boulders blocked the way. Alexis threaded the needle, sending the raft neatly between the two obstacles, over another ledge, and out the other side, where the river widened and flattened. But judging from the sounds up ahead, it was a momentary lull in the action. Sure enough, barely five minutes later, they were once more engulfed in white water, shooting forward through a narrow chute and then dodging around a whirling hole.

They went around a curve, and he spotted the tree Alexis had mentioned, a massive cottonwood blocking three-fourths of the river. Debris had piled up against it, caught against the branches, and Zeke hoped fervently they wouldn't be joining that debris pile. But Alexis easily dodged a rock to the right and then zipped across the water so that they could pass peacefully on the left of the tree into a series of ripples and rocks, which she navigated effortlessly as the river slowed and calmed. The way Alexis handled the raft reminded him of a video game he and his friends used to play as kids, where they'd jumped, dipped, spun, and dodged while obstacles and hazards attempted to do them in. Unlike a video game, though, this adventure didn't give each player multiple lives.

But Zeke realized he hadn't been any more afraid than he would have been on a roller coaster at an amusement park. Alexis was in command of the situation. It was clear, from the sparkle in her eyes as she handled the raft, that Alexis loved this. He'd seen that same sparkle when she was helping him with the cabin, examining how the logs fit together. She had a gift, a passion she carried with her for her work, her hobbies, and her relationships with people and with God.

She really was exceptional. Last night, when they'd kissed under the northern lights, Zeke felt as though he'd been given the most beautiful gift of all: a new beginning. He'd felt alive again—in a way he hadn't felt since the accident. For a little while at least, he'd been tempted to move on, to live his life and to see if he could find a way to bring Alexis into it.

But he'd had second thoughts. What right did he have to feel alive when Dani was dead? God had given him the love of a good woman and look how that ended. Zeke didn't deserve any woman's affection, especially not a woman as strong and kind and beautiful as Alexis.

In a few hours, they would be at Chapel Lake. Alexis and Keira would board a floatplane for Anchorage, and Zeke would never see them again. Which was exactly how it should be. He'd made the decision to live alone, to avoid relationships and the responsibility that went with them. That he had accepted responsibility for the lives of two special people when they wandered up to his cabin a few days ago didn't change his reasons or erase his past.

After talking to Alexis last night, he felt more at peace, but that didn't change the truth. He was better off alone, and the rest of the world was better off without him.

Once Alexis and Keira were safe, it was time to go back to his solitary life in the wilderness.

The current carried them along at a nice clip and oaring wasn't necessary, but Alexis oared anyway, giving them a little extra push toward the safety of Chapel Lake. They'd made it through the rapids and should be coming into view of the lake anytime now. And even though their floatplane wasn't due to pick them up for another five hours, she felt like once they'd reached the Chapel Lake Lodge, she could finally feel that Keira was safe.

She looked down at the patchwork raft with affection. It looked like a hot mess, but it had transported them through the rapids. Poppy had her front paws on the bow, looking out over the water as if she was watching for the first sign of roofs just like Alexis was. Behind her, Keira had her phone out again, snapping yet another picture of Denali in the distance. The mountain was especially lovely this morning, with only a few wispy clouds sticking to the sides and the snowy peak rising into the clear blue sky.

And then Alexis's eyes turned to Zeke, sitting back against the tube. He was watching the mountain as well, giving Alexis a minute to examine his face in profile. Not that she could see much of it behind the bushy beard, but she studied with affection those soft brown eyes with thick dark lashes, the strong nose, and the flash of white teeth as he laughed at something Keira said.

She had no doubt that Zeke had saved their freedom, and quite possibly their lives. Listening to him last night, she'd longed to take that heavy load of guilt and bear it for him, just for a little while. She wanted to make him understand that he was forgiven, that he had faced his past sins, but forgiveness wasn't hers to give. God's forgiveness was freely offered, but it had to be Zeke's decision to accept it.

It seemed like such a waste. Not for Zeke to build a cabin using century-old techniques—Alexis considered that a remarkable and valuable feat—but to isolate himself from people, to never share his gifts. Zeke was talented and intelligent with a subtle sense of humor she enjoyed. She was certain he was a wonderful physical therapist, encouraging and attentive, like he'd been with Keira.

Honestly, even if he hadn't rescued them, if Alexis had just gotten to know him from church or through a friend, she would have been attracted to him. At least the real him, not the solitary recluse he was pretending to be. As eager as she was to reach Chapel Lake Lodge, to put this whole terrifying week behind them, it would be hard to leave Zeke Soto behind.

The water slowed as the river began to spread at the inlet of the lake. They passed through a shady grove, and then there it was: Chapel Lake Lodge. It was nothing special architecturally, just a simple gabled building with fake log siding. But today, with the sun shining down on it like a spotlight, it was the most beautiful building Alexis had ever seen.

"There it is!" Keira shouted. She snapped a photo. "But I still can't get a cell signal."

"We're in a valley here and there's no tower," Alexis pointed out. "But the flight service told me in case there was a problem, we can find a pay phone in the lobby of the lodge."

"What's a pay phone?" Keira asked, with genuine curiosity.

Alexis exchanged amused glances with Zeke. "It's the latest technology. You'll be amazed."

"There's also a phone at the general store." Zeke waved a hand toward the Quonset hut that had been repurposed into a store, a ways down the shore from the lodge. "I know the guy who runs it. He takes messages for people coming and going, too."

Now that they were in the lake, the current no longer carried them along. Alexis spun the raft so that her back was toward the dock behind the lodge. She rowed steadily in that direction, feeling just a little safer with each stroke of her oars. Fifteen minutes later, they pulled up to the dock. Keira and Poppy jumped out, and Keira wrapped the bowline around a cleat.

Two men, one with thick gray hair and the other wearing a faded baseball cap, sat fishing on the far side of the dock. As Alexis and Zeke climbed out to join Keira on the dock, the fishermen eyed the multi-patched raft. "What do you suppose that's all about?" the one in the hat asked the other man in a voice that was probably louder than he realized.

"Grizzly, maybe?" his friend answered.

"What?" He cupped his hand to his ear.

"Grizzly bear tore it up, I'll bet," he shouted.

"Bet you're right." He cast his line out again.

Since neither of the men asked directly, Alexis decided there was no reason to enlighten them. She and Keira would no doubt be telling their story to the troopers at some point. She greeted the men and led Keira and Zeke toward the main lobby of the lodge. A sign directed them to a corner where the phone was set up, not exactly in a booth, but in a sort of alcove open to the rest of the room. This phone model took credit cards, which was nice because Alexis wasn't sure she had any quarters.

Alexis motioned for Keira to take the chair in front of the phone and slid her card through the slot. Dixon was supposed to return to Anchorage today, but she wasn't sure if he'd be there yet or if he would still be on his plane. She handed Keira the receiver. "Here. Call your mom."

"How?"

"You just dial the number. Dial 1 first."

"What number?"

Alexis laughed. "You don't know your own number?"

Keira looked offended. "I know mine. I just don't know Mom's. It's in my contacts. Oh, right. It's in my contacts." Keira pulled out her cell phone and, after looking it up, managed to make the call. "Mom?"

Alexis left Keira alone to tell her mother the story and wandered back to the lobby, where Zeke stood in front of a record-setting Coho salmon mount on the wall. She studied the huge red-and-green fish. "That bear we passed would have made a good meal out of this one."

"Judging by the size of that bear, he hasn't missed too many meals. Must be a good fisherman." Zeke jerked his head toward the phone alcove. "She okay?"

Alexis nodded. "I think so. She's talking to her mother. Why?"

"I don't know. She just had a funny look on her face when you were walking away."

Alexis looked back, but now Keira was rolling her eyes, an expression Alexis was far too familiar with. Keira motioned for Alexis to come back. "Mom wants to talk to you."

"Okay." Alexis picked up the phone.

Before Alexis could even say hello, Mara started in. "I cannot believe this. I told Dixon this was a bad idea, that Keira was too young. He said you used to go with your dad when you were younger than Keira, but just because your father was willing to submit you to danger doesn't mean it's okay for you to endanger my daughter."

"Now hold on. The danger Keira faced had nothing to do with the float trip. It was—"

"I don't want to hear your excuses. I need my daughter home safe."

Fair enough. "The floatplane is scheduled to pick us up at three. I left my car at Lake Hood, so I'll bring her straight home as soon as we get to Anchorage."

"That's not for five hours." The panic in her voice was surprising. Mara didn't usually spend that much emotional energy on things that didn't directly affect her.

Alexis was immediately ashamed of that thought. Mara was Keira's mother, after all. "I know, but we'll hang around here at the lodge in the meantime. We'll be fine. And I can give the troopers a call, see if they want to meet us in Anchorage or fly out here."

"Don't do that," Mara ordered.

"What?"

"Don't call the troopers. You've already traumatized my daughter enough."

Alexis looked over at Keira, who was standing to the side, listening. She looked more annoyed than traumatized. "Keira's handling this well. I'm proud of her." Her words were for Keira as well as her mother.

But Mara wasn't reassured. "I don't want her interrogated by a bunch of policemen without me. She needs to come home."

Alexis could see her point, but the more time they wasted, the less likely it was that the kidnappers would be caught. "We have to report this."

"Not until Keira is here, where I can take care of her."

"Okay." Alexis had never witnessed Mara acting quite like this, but then they'd never had an attempted kidnapping before. "If the plane is on time, we should be back at the dock by four, and I'll have her home to you by four thirty."

"No, I'm not waiting that long. I'll send someone there to pick her up now."

"That's really not necess—"

"Stay at this number. I'll call you back as soon as I make arrangements."

"Fine. But I don't see—" The phone disconnected. Alexis looked at the receiver for a moment before returning it to the hook. She and Keira's mom had never been best friends, but they'd always been cor dial. She just hoped this didn't mean she wouldn't be able to spend as much time with Keira in the future. Their time together depended on her mother's approval.

Alexis straightened her shoulders. She would just have to do whatever it took to reassure Mara that Keira would be safe with her. The kidnappers had already done enough harm. Alexis wasn't going to let them damage her relationship with her niece, too. She turned to Keira, who was frowning down at the planks of the floor. "What's wrong?" Alexis asked.

"I don't know," Keira answered. "Mom's acting weird."

"Weird, how?"

"She was like—" Keira switched her voice to a falsetto "—'Oh, my gosh. I'm so scared for my precious baby girl.'" Keira returned to her normal voice. "She never talks like that."

"Well, people react in different ways under stress. Once she sees that you're okay, she'll probably feel better."

"I hope so," Keira huffed. She went to stand next to Zeke and the fish. She must have made some funny remark about it, because Zeke laughed.

Ten minutes later, the pay phone rang, and Alexis answered.

"I found a pilot. He'll pick you and Keira up at the lodge in an hour. He'll be flying an Otter."

The Otter was a bigger plane than they needed, but Alexis supposed that wasn't important. "Thank you. I'll get everything ready for pickup and we'll see you soon. Do you want to talk to Keira again?"

"No. That's all right. I'll meet her at Lake Hood and take her home."

"Okay." Alexis hung up and then called the flying service to cancel their originally scheduled floatplane. Once that was accomplished, she joined Keira and Zeke. "Your mom has arranged for a plane to pick us up in an hour, so I guess we'd better get the raft broken down and packed up."

"I thought you already had a plane scheduled at three," Zeke said.

"I did, but she was insistent she could get one here sooner, so…" Alexis shrugged.

"Okay, then. Let's get you packed." The words sounded eager, but when Alexis stole a glance his way, she saw sadness in his eyes. Maybe he'd miss them, too.

Chapter Fourteen

Between the three of them, it didn't take long to disassemble the oar frames, deflate the raft and roll the pieces together into a bundle that would fit neatly into the plane. Not that Alexis ever planned to use the patched raft again, but she might as well take it back to Anchorage for disposal. All their gear was stacked on one side of the dock, ready to load.

The two fishermen who had been there earlier had wandered off, leaving the three of them alone on the dock, but there were people eating lunch on the lodge's second-story deck that overlooked the area. A family with two little boys were picnicking at a table not far away, near the lake. A Steller's jay swooped down to the table, snatched something from a plate and flew away, leaving an outraged toddler in his wake.

Keira laughed, but seeing the picnic must have triggered her appetite. "I'm hungry."

Alexis looked at her watch. They really didn't have time to eat at the lodge restaurant before the plane was due to land. "We'll be back in Anchorage in an hour and a half. Would an energy bar hold you until then?" Alexis glanced at their gear. Naturally, the bag with the energy bars was at the bottom of the stack.

"I'd rather have a muffin and hot chocolate from the coffee bar in the lodge," Keira suggested, her eyes wide and hopeful.

"Good idea." Alexis dug some cash from the wallet in her backpack. "Bring me a muffin and a coffee, please. Zeke, what would you like?"

"Nothing for me."

Keira trotted off into the lodge. Alexis watched until she was through the doors and then turned to Zeke. It felt wrong, leaving him here after all he had done for them. She had to try. "Will you come with us to Anchorage?"

"No." He didn't meet her eyes. "You'll be all right now." He'd been like this since they'd arrived, distant, unwilling to look at her. Last night, she'd felt like they'd bonded, but maybe that was the problem. Maybe he'd let her learn more than he'd intended, and now he regretted it.

She decided not to push. "How will you get back to the cabin?"

"I know someone here who owns a floatplane. He'll drop me at Pearson Lake, and I can take a water taxi from there."

Alexis took more cash from her wallet and handed it to Zeke.

He frowned. "What's this for?"

"To cover the cost of the plane and boat."

"That's not necessary." He tried to return the cash, but she held her hand over his to stop him.

"You've done so much for us. Please let me do this small thing."

He hesitated, but accepted the money. "Thank you."

"Thank you, Zeke. For everything." Alexis pulled a business card from her wallet, and after locating a pen in her pack, she scribbled her address and cell number on the back. "Please, when you get back to Anchorage, give me a call." She held out the card.

He shook his head. "I don't think so."

"You don't think you'll ever get back to Anchorage, or you won't be calling me?"

"Either. Both." He finally met her eyes. "You don't owe me anything, Alexis. I won't be tracking you down, looking for payment."

He still didn't get it. "I might possibly owe you my life, and Keira's, too, but that's not why I gave you my number. I care about you, Zeke, and I'd love to see you again. Is that so wrong of me?"

"No." He gave a long sigh. "But I believe it's better if you don't. I'm not really fit to be around people."

How could he say that? She'd seen the kind of man he was, not only someone who would risk his own life and property for someone else, but who could build a cabin and joke with an almost-teenager and knew just the right spot to rub an old dog's belly. "I disagree, but I'll respect your decision. However, if you ever, and I do mean ever, change your mind, I want to hear from you. Even if it's just a postcard."

He nodded and stashed the card in his pocket before pulling his backpack onto his shoulders.

"Then I guess this is goodbye and thank you once again." It felt so inadequate. She should be throwing a parade for the man or giving him a medal, but this would have to do. But she wouldn't let him go without a hug. She put her arms around him and held him tight, and slowly, she felt his arms steal around her as well. She laid her cheek against his shoulder, and then looked up to see him looking at her with such softness in his eyes, she couldn't resist rising on her toes for one more kiss. Her lips brushed his. He hesitated for an instant and then leaned in for a lingering, heart-tugging kiss, filled with the pain of a final goodbye.

He raised his head, and for a long moment, they locked eyes and said nothing, as though neither of them wanted to break the spell. But finally, Zeke closed his eyes, breathed in a shaky breath and stepped back. "Take care of yourself, Alexis. I'll stop and say goodbye to Keira on my way through the lodge."

She watched him walk away. How could a man she hadn't even known existed a week ago leave such a big hole in his wake?

* * *

Keira was still debating the merits of blueberry muffins versus lemon scones when Zeke spotted her in the lobby. He leaned in and whispered, "Get both. You know you'll be hungry again in an hour."

Keira laughed. "Two muffins and one scone, please." She turned to Zeke. "You sure you don't want anything?"

There was so much he wanted, starting with a relationship with her aunt, but he didn't deserve any of it. "I'm good. Listen, I'm taking off, so I wanted to say goodbye."

Keira's eyes widened. "You're leaving?"

"Yeah. I need to make arrangements to get back to my cabin."

Her lower lip trembled. "I'll miss you."

"I'll miss you, too," he answered honestly. "Both of you."

"Will I see you again?" Her direct gaze demanded an honest answer.

"Probably not. But I'll never forget you." He rested an arm on her shoulders. "You're going to be great in middle school, Tejónita. Just remember to stand your ground. Okay?"

She nodded, her eyes misty. "Okay."

"'Bye, Keira. Take care." He gave her shoulders a squeeze and turned to walk out before he changed his mind and returned to Alexis, begging to be allowed on that plane back to Anchorage.

He walked along the road that paralleled the

shoreline, knowing he would find Roger at the general store. Roger was an old friend from his piloting days, pretty much the only one he was still in any contact with. After the crash, several of his friends and coworkers had sent cards or stopped by the rehab center, and then, good deed done, they'd moved on. Not that he'd given them any reason to turn up again. But every Tuesday, while in Anchorage on his weekly resupply run, Roger would stop by to talk. And more importantly, to listen.

When Zeke had declared he would never fly again, Roger hadn't argued. When Zeke had told him he was quitting his job, Roger had been concerned, but he understood. When Zeke confessed he was having trouble praying, Roger said he was praying for both of them. And when Zeke had bought the land and told Roger he planned to build a cabin on it, Roger had flown him and his supplies to Pearson Lake.

As he reached an opening in the woods, Zeke spotted Roger's familiar orange floatplane at the dock down the hill from the general store. Roger was one of the best pilots Zeke knew. He respected his limits and would never have taken a plane into that weather system like Zeke had, hoping to thread the needle. If Roger had been her pilot, Dani would still be alive. But it was too late to change any of that.

Zeke hoped Roger's wife, Bette, would be available to cover the store for an hour or so at some point, so that Roger could duck out and fly Zeke to Pearson Lake. Otherwise, he'd have to wait until the store closed. Which was no big deal, either, since the days were still long, and he had no burning reason to return. For the first time in a long time, he wasn't feeling desperate to separate himself from other people.

He hadn't talked to his friend since April, when Roger had dropped off the last load of supplies and told him he'd be praying for him. He'd confided to Roger his hope that living in the wilderness would bring him closer to God. Now he would have to confess that it really hadn't had that effect...except, maybe it had. This morning, when he saw Alexis mouthing her prayer for guidance before she'd entered the rapids, he'd been praying right along with her. And for the first time in a long time, he'd felt that his prayer was heard and answered. Maybe when Zeke had chosen to take responsibility for Alexis and Keira's safety, he'd aligned himself with God's will. It was a heady thought, the idea that he and God were on the same side. That God was working through him.

Zeke reached the store, and after holding the door for a woman coming out with two bags in one arm and a husky puppy in the other, he went inside. Bette was at the register, ringing up purchases while catching up with the local gossip. Two young men, one with a baby in a carrier on his chest, chatted as they gathered their groceries. A woman with gray braids sorted through a pile of apples, examining them one at a time and returning them to the pile.

Over in one corner, a burly man in his fifties cast an eye over the selection of fishing flies, but none of them seemed to catch his interest. Roger was at the back, on the pay phone. After a moment, he turned and called, "Anybody here named Jack? Jack Sampson? No?" He turned back to the phone, mumbled something and wrote something on the notepad beside the phone. He tore off the page, folded it in half and wrote *Jack from Leila* on the front. He pinned it to the corkboard beside the phone that already held two other messages in Roger's bold writing, *Steve from Sierra Air* and *Vic from Mara*. He looked up and spotted Zeke. "Woo! Look what the cat dragged in. Good to see you, man!" And suddenly Zeke was enveloped in a bear hug.

He hugged his friend back and thumped him on the shoulder. "You, too. Busy, I see."

"Always. How is life treating you these days?"

As soon as Roger stepped away, the man from the fishing section squeezed past them, snatched one of the messages off the board and opened it. Stuffing the note in his pocket, he bumped into Roger in his hurry to dash from the store.

"Oh, excuse me for standing in your way, and you're welcome," Roger called after him. Then he turned to Zeke, a smile on his face. "It's good to see you alive and well. What brings you here? On your way to Anchorage?"

"No. Long story, but I need to get back to the cabin," Zeke told him. "Wondered if you might be available to fly me to Pearson Lake sometime today." He thought he saw a flicker of disappointment cross Roger's face, but it was gone so quickly he couldn't be sure.

"Yeah, of course," Roger said. "But not for a couple hours. I've got a guy coming by soon to give me an estimate on adding a storeroom to the back. But here—" Roger reached into his pocket, pulled out an overcrowded key ring and removed one of the keys. "You go get the plane gassed up and ready. Tell them to put it on my account."

"That's okay. I have cash for gas," Zeke told him, remembering the money Alexis had insisted he take, which was good since he didn't have an account at the gas pumps here.

"Even better. I'll meet you at the plane dock, then." Someone who had come in asked Roger if he carried bug armor, and he went to show them his extensive selection of net head covers.

Zeke waved at Bette, who was busy ringing up another customer, and started for the door, but before he reached it, Bette called, "Hold it right there, mister. You're not going anywhere without a hug."

He grinned and waited while she finished with her customer and the one waiting behind him, and then waved Zeke over and wrapped her arms around him. Barely five feet tall, Bette still gave fierce hugs. Once she'd released him, she patted his beard. "Nice mountain-man vibe you've got going on there. How is the cabin coming along?"

"Good. I already built a little one I'm living in now, and I've almost reached the top of the walls for the main cabin."

"I'm glad. I saw Roger give you the keys. Are you flying the plane?" Her voice was hopeful.

"No." Zeke would never pilot another plane. "Roger asked me to gas up the plane so he can fly me to Pearson Lake. I need to get back to my cabin-building."

"I see." She searched his eyes, and Zeke was afraid she was going to demand a full report on his relationship with God, but instead she patted his face and let him go. A woman standing at the register cleared her throat, but Bette waved her off. "Be there in a jiff." She gave Zeke a smile. "You take care of yourself, you hear?"

"I will. You, too, Bette."

"Okay." She gave his shoulder one final pat and returned to the register.

Zeke made his way around to the deck behind the store, where Roger had set up a few picnic tables for customers. Dark spruce trees covered the hillside below him to the edge of the blue water. He took the path leading down from the store that would pass by Roger and Bette's snug little cabin and on to the dock at the end of the peninsula. It formed one edge of the cove where the floatplane would be parked.

In a couple of hours, Zeke would be going home. Home. He pondered on that concept. Somehow the cabins he'd so carefully crafted had never been a home, not until a week ago when Alexis and Keira had shown up out of the blue and changed everything. But now his time with them was over, and he needed to get back into his routine, to remember the reasons he'd chosen to live alone.

But somehow the reasons seemed fuzzier than they had been before. An image of Dani's face smiling up at him flashed in his memory. Alexis was right. He had lots of good memories of Dani and their time together. Perhaps instead of focusing on her death, it was more important to honor her life and the person she was.

He reached the dock where the familiar orange floatplane was tethered. It was a Super Cub, the same model as the one Zeke and his coworkers had purchased together. The one he crashed. A good reminder of why he shouldn't be responsible for anyone but himself.

He climbed into the plane. It was his first time in the pilot seat since the accident, and a surge of panic twisted in his gut as his gaze fell on the familiar dials and gauges. His heart rate jumped into overdrive. He took a deep, calming breath. He wasn't going to fly, just taxi across the lake and gas up the plane. No pressure.

As a calming measure, he started the preflight check. Or more accurately, the pre-preflight check, since Roger would of course be doing it again. Control lock removed, ignition off, avionics off, master switch off, flaps down. Fuel was low, but he would be taking care of that in a few minutes once he'd regained his composure. As he went through the rest of the checklist, his equilibrium returned. The plane was sound. The weather was clear. And all he had to do was cross the lake, fill the tank and return to the dock. Roger would do the flying.

Once he'd completed the checklist, Zeke taxied across the lake to the gas pumps. As he arrived, the man from Roger's store was just following another guy into a de Havilland Otter. Big plane for two people plus a pilot, but maybe they had lots of gear. Zeke pulled into the slot the Otter left behind and filled the tanks. Once he'd paid for the gas, he returned the plane to Roger's dock and tied it to the cleat.

The Otter had taxied across the lake toward the dock at the lodge. Because the lodge's dock and Roger's dock were both on points of land that extended into the lake, they were only about fifty yards apart even though the curved shoreline that connected them was easily four times that. Alexis, Keira and Poppy waited on the dock, beside the pile of gear. Now the larger plane made more sense. Keira's mother had probably arranged for them to join an already scheduled party, and that was how she'd gotten a plane to them so quickly. Based on Alexis's description and a few things Keira had mentioned, Zeke's feelings toward Keira's mother weren't the warmest, but she had his sympathy today. After hearing about the attempted kidnapping, it was no wonder she wanted her daughter home as quickly as possible.

The pilot got out of the plane and said something to Alexis. She nodded, grabbed a couple of bags from the top of the pile and handed them to him to load. The other two men remained in the back seat of the plane, apparently not inclined to get out and assist. Zeke debated going to help, but by the time he'd picked his way along the winding shoreline trail, they'd probably be finished. Besides, saying goodbye had been painful enough without doing it twice. Keira and Alexis would be safe in Anchorage soon, and that was the important thing.

And then it hit him—Mara.

The message the man had picked up at the store was to *Vic from Mara*. Of course, that proved nothing; there were plenty of Maras in the world. Even if this Mara was Keira's mother, it might have had something to do with sharing the plane. But the note, coupled with the small number of people who knew Alexis was taking Keira on this rafting trip and her mother's grievance about the divorce settlement, suggested a dangerous possibility.

Alexis had just boosted Poppy into the plane and bent to grab another dry bag. If Zeke was wrong, no harm done. But if he was right…

Zeke took a deep breath, held his hands to his mouth to form a megaphone and yelled at the top of his lungs, "Alexis. Don't get on that plane!"

Her head shot up. She looked his direction and gestured that she didn't understand what he'd said.

He yelled again. "Don't get on the plane. It's the kidnappers! Run!"

She wheeled toward Keira, but the pilot, who had been loading the plane, shoved Alexis hard enough to send her splashing into the lake. Before Keira could react, he'd grabbed her and stuffed her onto the plane with the help of the men inside. People from the second-story deck of the lodge yelled something, but they were too far away to help. Zeke took off at a dead run along the trail that lined the edge of the cove, but long before he could get anywhere near the lodge dock, the yellow plane had taxied to the middle of the lake.

He ran to the dock and pulled Alexis out of the water, but it was too late to stop the plane with Keira aboard. It was already taking off.

Chapter Fifteen

"**A**re you all right?" Zeke looked Alexis up and down, but other than drenched clothes, she seemed okay.

"I'm fine. But Keira—"

"I saw. Come on." Zeke grabbed her hand and tugged her along the path he'd just traversed.

"Where are we going?" Alexis was trying to keep pace while watching the yellow plane in the sky grow smaller. "Shouldn't we report this to someone?"

"I'm sure the witnesses from the lodge will call it in, but we'll do it, too. From the air. My friend has a plane." And Roger was an excellent pilot. Briefly Zeke considered running up the hill to get him, but the more time that passed, the less likely it was that they could follow the flight path of the yellow Otter. "I'm going to fly it."

Alexis didn't question his decision. She ran with him until they reached the dock and followed him into the Piper. Zeke sat in the pilot's seat, glad he'd already gone through the preflight check. Before he started the ignition, he spared one glance at Alexis's beautiful face, now pale with fear. He tried for a smile. "Now might be a good time for a prayer."

She reached for his arm and gave it a squeeze. "You fly. I'll pray."

And she did, quietly but earnestly as he checked the switches and controls. A hard lump of terror sat in the middle of his stomach, trying to fight its way to the surface, but he pushed it down. He didn't have time to be afraid. Keira needed him. And this time, that inner voice told him it was the right thing to do. He taxied to the middle of the lake, took a deep breath, and suddenly the fear melted away, replaced by a deep and profound sense of peace. God was with him today. "Guide me, Lord," he murmured just before he accelerated.

The plane raced across the water, gaining velocity, shaking with the chop, until they'd reached the speed where, with a slight adjustment, he could lift one float from the lake and then the other, breaking free from the surface and jumping into the air. He pulled back on the stick, gaining altitude until they were high above the lake. The blue water looked deceptively peaceful, as though nothing like violence or kidnapping could ever happen in such a place. But it had.

"Can you see the plane?" Zeke asked.

"No, but they went that way," Alexis answered, pointing toward the mountain pass to the east.

Zeke pointed the nose in that direction, hoping to get through the pass before the Otter was completely out of sight. Roger's Piper had a top speed slightly faster than that of the Otter, but if they wasted much time flying in circles, they would lose that advantage.

"How did you know the kidnappers were in that plane?" Alexis asked.

He explained about the note from Mara. "And then, when I realized the other two passengers were hiding in the plane so you wouldn't recognize them, it all clicked."

Alexis stared. "You're saying Mara is behind this kidnapping?"

"I'm afraid so. You told me yourself that she's bitter about the divorce settlement. She must see this as a way to get the money she believes should be rightfully hers."

"But to do that to her own daughter—"

"I know. The good news is, if Keira's mother is behind this, the kidnappers probably have strict orders not to harm Keira."

Alexis nodded slowly. "I guess that's something, but still—Keira must be beyond frightened. How could anyone justify terrorizing a child, any child, much less her own?"

"I don't know. I guess sometimes people get so wrapped up in their own selfish desires, other people just aren't real to them. They're just pawns to be manipulated and used."

Alexis thought for a moment. "I saw some of that, right after the divorce. Mara would purposely make visitation as difficult and inconvenient as possible for Dixon. She would make appointments, change them at the last minute, and then claim he was neglectful if he didn't agree to the change. Not that there wasn't a kernel of truth in it. He is too focused on the business, but—" Alexis sighed. "I thought things had gotten better between them, but Mara must have been nursing this grievance until it ate her up inside to the point where she can't even see right and wrong."

They had flown through the pass, and the sky opened up in front of them. "Do you see any sign of the other plane?" Zeke asked.

"No." Alexis bit her lip as she scanned the sky. "Let's try that way." She pointed toward the northeast, in the direction where the mountains sloped down toward another drainage.

Zeke banked to the left without questioning her decision. One guess was as good as another, and maybe this was an answer to a prayer. He picked up his radio. "I'll call this in to the troopers."

"Wait. Won't they be able to overhear in the other plane if you do?"

"Good point." They didn't want the kidnappers to know they were on their tail.

"Let me see if I can get a cell signal instead."

Alexis pulled her phone from her pocket and powered it up. Almost instantly, text notifications began chiming, one after another. Before Alexis could open her text app, the phone rang. "It's Dixon! Hello?"

She paused for a moment, listening. "It's not a hoax. They followed us to Leah Falls. Keira got away that day, but they've been trying ever since. They snatched her at the Chapel Lake Lodge dock a little while ago and took her in a yellow de Havilland Otter…No, I didn't notice the tail number. Listen, Dixon, I'm in a floatplane with a friend. We took off a few minutes after they did, and we're trying to follow them. They're not in sight, but we're up here looking." She listened. "Yes, please report it to the troopers right away. We're currently at— Hold on." She checked the GPS coordinates on her phone and read them off to her brother.

Another text alert chimed on her phone. "She's doing what? Oh, Keira, you are brilliant!" Alexis exclaimed. "I'll call right back, Dixon." Alexis looked at her text messages. "She's sending Dixon, me and two of her friends the coordinates as they go. They must not have figured out she's using her phone yet."

"Impressive! That shows some amazing presence of mind. I believe Keira takes after her aunt in that regard."

Alexis tossed him a short grin. "I don't know about that, but she is incredible." She paused to read off the coordinates of the latest text, and Zeke adjusted his course. It wasn't far off from the direction they'd already been traveling. Alexis chewed on her bottom lip. "I didn't tell Dixon our suspicions about Mara yet. I guess I should."

Zeke nodded. "I'd imagine the more information he can give the troopers, the better. It's interesting that Keira didn't include her mother on the text chain."

"That is interesting. I wonder if one of the kidnappers let something slip. Anyway, I'd better alert Dixon." She started to redial, but before she could, her phone rang again. "It's Sarah's mother. That's one of Keira's best friends. Hello, Rachel." She listened. "Yes, it's real. Dixon is notifying the troopers right now." She listened for a moment. "Absolutely. The more prayers, the better. I will let you know as soon as we find her. Thanks, Rachel."

Alexis turned to Zeke. "She's praying."

"I heard. So am I."

"I know. Zeke, thank you for this. I know it must be difficult for you to fly."

"You know, it was, but then it wasn't. It was like a weight was lifted off my shoulders so I could do what I needed to do."

She nodded, as though she wasn't surprised. Another text popped up, and she read off the coordinates. They seemed to be following the river. "I'll call Dixon back." When her brother answered, she dived right in. "Listen, I don't know how to say this, but I'm afraid Mara might be involved." She explained their reasoning, and then listened, shak-

ing her head. "Weird. Okay, Dixon, I'm getting another call. I think it's the troopers."

Before she answered, she told Zeke, "Mara's disappeared. She's not answering her cell, and when
Dixon called the landline, her housekeeper said she
thought Mara had gone on a cruise, but the cruise
line says she canceled last week." She answered the
phone. "Alexis Mahoney...Yes, I have Zeke Soto with
me, flying the plane. I'll put you on speaker."

"I understand you're following the abductor's
plane," the voice on the phone said. "Do you have
it in sight?"

"Negative," Zeke answered. "But the GPS coordinates we're following appear to be leading us along
this river valley."

"The Niptaitchuk River, according to my maps,"
Alexis volunteered.

"Good, that helps. If you sight the plane, please
report but do not pursue."

"But we—" Alexis protested.

"Repeat—do not pursue. We'll have people in the
air within the hour. We—" The words garbled, and
then stopped.

"The call dropped," Alexis said.

Zeke motioned toward a mountain peak to the
southeast. "Signal shadow. We'll probably pick it up
in a bit." He continued to follow the valley, keeping
an eye out for the yellow plane, but other than a few
birds, the skies were clear. Surely, they hadn't lost

the trail completely. Fifteen minutes later, Alexis's phone chimed with another text.

"Is that another set of coordinates?"

"Yes, sent ten minutes ago. Oh, no. We've already gone past this one."

"That's okay." Zeke banked to turn the plane back the way they'd come. Far in the distance, he thought he saw a speck against the sky. "Look. Do you see it?"

Alexis squinted. "Oh, I do. It's yellow!"

"And it's climbing."

"How did it turn around and get past us without us seeing it?"

"It must have landed and taken off."

"The troopers said not to pursue." Alexis looked at Zeke doubtfully.

He nodded. "We won't want to, anyway. Because if the plane landed and took off—"

"It was probably dropping Keira and the kidnappers somewhere." She scanned the land below them. "But where?"

"We know it was in this general area. It had to be a lake, or at least a wide, calm spot in the river. Keep an eye out."

"There's a lake," Alexis pointed out.

"Okay, I'm going to fly by, but not too low. We don't want to alert them that we know they're there. Keep your eyes peeled for any sign of people." He made a wide sweep to give Alexis the best view of the shoreline possible without getting too close.

"There!" She pointed. "I see a cabin with a dock. I'm dropping a pin on my map."

"Can you get a call off to the troopers?"

"No, we're still in the signal shadow."

Zeke scouted the area. "The lake bends so that the upper lake is out of sight from the lower part, and the wind is blowing upstream, so our engine noise would carry away from the cabin. We could send the troopers the cabin coordinates and then set the plane down there. We should be able to make our way along the shoreline to check out the cabin. If Keira's not there, we can tell the troopers so they won't waste their time on a wild-goose chase. If she is—"

"Then maybe we can find a way to rescue her, or at least keep an eye on the situation to make sure they don't move her."

"I have to warn you, though, there's always a danger in setting down on an unfamiliar lake. From what I can see, there are no sandbars or submerged logs under the water, but I can't guarantee your safety."

She locked her eyes on him. "I trust your judgment."

He shook his head, doubts bubbling. "You know what happened before."

"I do. And that's why I trust you now. I know you'll weigh the situation carefully and won't take any unnecessary risks. Can you do it?"

From high above, he made another pass over the upper lake. The shallow ridges on the sides stood out clearly, but the wide middle looked to be as clear and unobstructed as a landing strip. A sandy length of beach on one side would be an easy place to dock. He nodded. "Yes."

"Then let's land."

"Okay. Put the cabin coordinates in a text, and as soon as we pass out of the signal shadow, send it off to the troopers. Then we'll turn around and set down."

While they flew up the valley past the signal-blocking peak, Alexis composed the text. "Should I tell them we're landing on the upper lake?"

"We should, just so when they see the orange plane, they'll know it's ours."

She tilted her head. "They might tell us not to go."

Zeke grinned. "We'll be out of cell phone range before they can tell us anything."

"Good point." Alexis finished the text, and the second her phone registered a signal, she sent it off. There were no more GPS texts from Keira, but then if she was at the cabin in the signal shadow, there wouldn't be. Zeke turned the plane and headed back toward the lake.

A moderate wind blew upstream, exactly in the direction he needed to land, but not hard enough to create a lot of chop in the water. No obstacles, animals or other hazards seemed to be in the way. Landing and takeoff were always the most danger-ous parts of flight, but conditions were as good as they got for a floatplane. With God's help, he could do this. "Guide me, Lord."

He eased the plane down, down. The left float touched and then the right, and the plane tucked onto the water like a duck. Zeke let out the breath he hadn't realized he was holding. "Thank You, God."

Alexis reached across to give his shoulder a squeeze. "Amen."

Chapter Sixteen

Alexis swept her gaze around the lakeshore, but there was no sign of anyone who might have witnessed their landing. It looked like more than a mile of heavy forest between this part of the lake and the area where she'd spotted the cabin, so the kidnappers shouldn't be expecting them. Zeke taxied to the sandy beach along part of the shore. Alexis pointed to a little cove with overhanging trees. "We could leave the plane there, and no one would spot it from the lake."

"Good idea." Zeke motored into the cove and cut the engine, allowing their momentum to carry them toward the shore. Alexis opened the door and climbed onto one of the floats.

"Wait. I'll hop out and drag us closer so that you don't need to get your feet wet," Zeke offered.

Despite her fears for Keira, Alexis chuckled. "I'm already soaked from my first dunking. Let me do it." She grabbed a mooring line, waded through the shallow water and tethered the plane to a mature spruce tree.

Zeke grabbed his backpack and joined her on the bank. "Are you ready to check out that cabin?"

Was she? The troopers were on the way, and it could be argued that if they were holding Keira at the cabin, hostage negotiation should be left to the experts. But the thought of Keira, scared and alone with the kidnappers, drove Alexis to do something. If they were right and Mara was behind this, the kidnappers probably had strict instructions not to harm Keira, but if they were cornered, who knew what they would do? At the very least, she and Zeke could keep an eye on the cabin while they waited for the troopers. Alexis straightened her shoulders. "Let's go."

She followed Zeke along the game trail that paralleled the lakeshore, trying to emulate his ability to move silently through the woods. If she could have anyone in the world with her right now, Zeke would always be her first choice. His intelligence, common sense, and the dedication to keeping Keira safe that he'd shown since the very first day made him the man she trusted most.

She'd thought, there at the dock on Chapel Lake, that she would never see him again, even though letting him go had been one of the hardest things she'd ever done. But the moment he sensed danger, Zeke had come running back. He'd conquered his fear and guilt in order to fly the airplane, because he was more invested in saving Keira than he was in his own tragedy. He might never believe it, but Alexis knew it was so: Zeke was a true hero.

They passed an area where a strong wind had blown some trees over in the past year or so. Zeke detoured off the trail to show her how the shallow-rooted birches had gone down, roots and all, leaving small caverns underneath. Ferns and grasses were growing up around them, all but hiding the hollows. "A good place to hide out, if we need it," he pointed out.

"Good to know." They resumed their trek. As they neared the clearing around the cabin, Zeke slowed beside a huge boulder and waited for her to catch up. "Why don't you circle around to the mountain side of the cabin while I check out the lake side? Keep out of sight. Then we'll meet back here to confer."

"Sounds good." Alexis crept forward. Fortunately, second growth had sprouted around the edges of the cleared area near the cabin, creating a thick screen of foliage between her and the cabin. The cabin itself looked as though it had been built in the last few years. It was one level with a simple gabled design. Only one window looked out from this side of the house, near the back, and it was covered with storm shutters latched from the outside. The shutters were open on the two windows that faced the front porch, and there were no windows in the back, only a door with a covered stoop. Low-maintenance siding in a silvered gray designed to look like weathered wood covered the outer walls, with a darker gray metal roof.

It had no doubt gone up much faster than Zeke's cabin, but she doubted it would last as long. Like Zeke's property, though, it boasted a well-stocked woodpile out back adjacent to a matching outhouse behind and downhill of the main cabin, partially hidden by a shrubby mountain ash. It was hard to tell if the cabin was occupied. Alexis thought she might hear voices, but that could just be the murmur of the lake. Maybe Zeke could tell.

She was working her way back toward the rendezvous spot when she thought she heard a bark. She stopped to listen, and it came again. Yes! That was Poppy's warning bark, the one she used from inside the house when she spotted a moose in the yard. If Poppy was there, so was Keira. But Poppy's bark also meant she was feeling the need to protect Keira from something, and Alexis didn't like that at all.

When she got to the rock, Zeke was already waiting. "That was Poppy, right?"

"Yes. And she wasn't happy." Alexis paced a few steps and turned. "I don't think we should wait for the troopers. Who knows how long it could be before they're here and in position? The longer these guys have Keira, the more opportunity for something to go wrong."

"I agree, but rushing in might be even more dangerous. I don't want to use guns."

Alexis gulped at the idea of Keira caught in the middle. "Agreed."

After exchanging information about the layout on both sides of the cabin, Zeke thought for a few moments. "There appeared to be two men in the plane in addition to the pilot, presumably the same two men I saw in the boat on Pearson River. They could have someone else who waited here, but I would think the fewer people involved in a criminal operation, the less risky it would be. So since the plane is gone, I'm guessing it's just those two."

"Yes." That made sense.

"If we could pick them off separately—"

"The outhouse," Alexis suggested. "It's out of direct sight from the cabin, and if they're nervous, and how could they not be, someone will surely need to use it before long. Maybe even Keira."

"That'll work."

Zeke removed a hank of rope from his backpack and they made their way closer to the cabin. He positioned himself behind the woodpile where he would be out of sight from the door of the outhouse. Alexis went farther into the woods, behind a thick bush, where she could keep an eye on both the outhouse and the back door. Time crept by, but according to her phone, they'd been waiting less than half an hour when the back door opened.

The man with familiar orange hiking boots stepped outside. Now that she could see his face, Alexis realized he was younger than she'd assumed, around nineteen or twenty; he had a lanky build. Zeke probably had two inches of height and a good forty pounds on him. "Going to take care of some personal business," he called toward the cabin. "Be back in a minute." Another male voice answered, but she couldn't understand the words. Orange Boots must have, though, because she saw his eyes roll. "I will when I get back."

Poppy barked again somewhere inside and came running to try to squeeze out the door before he could shut it behind him. *No, Poppy.* Alexis silently pleaded with the dog. *Don't give us away.* The man shoved her back inside and shut the door behind him. He walked directly to the outhouse without looking around, so apparently he didn't expect company. Once he was inside with the door shut, Alexis signaled Zeke. Silently, they arranged themselves on both sides of the outhouse door, hidden by the mountain ash just in case the other man should look out the back door.

Orange Boots didn't seem to be in any hurry, but eventually he opened the door and stepped outside, still buckling his belt. Before he'd realized what was happening, Zeke had stepped up behind him, slapped one hand over his mouth and the other round his shoulders, and dragged him farther into the woods. When Alexis came up in front of them, holding the rope, the young man's eyes widened and he ceased struggling.

Zeke didn't remove his hand from the man's mouth until they were a good distance from the cabin. As soon as he did, the kidnapper started babbling. "It wasn't me. I didn't want to do any of this. It was my uncle, Victor. My mom lives with him, and he said if I didn't help him, he'd kick her out on the street. She was homeless once before and I couldn't let that happen again. He made me do it. I swear."

"What's your name?" Alexis asked.

"Brant. Brant Cooper. I've never done anything like this before. For real."

"I'm sure the troopers will want to hear all about this," Zeke told him as he tied his hands behind his back, "but right now we're more interested in what's going on in the cabin. How many people are there?"

"Just Uncle Vic and the girl, Keira. She's not hurt or anything. She's pretty mad because when she wouldn't give Vic her security code, he threw her phone in the lake, but she's okay."

If he didn't have the code, he wouldn't know about the messages Keira had been sending. Alexis was once more impressed with her niece. "Where in the cabin is she?"

"Vic has her locked in the bedroom, the one at the back on the side away from the lake. He's in the front room."

Zeke tied Brant's ankles together so that he could walk, but slowly. "Is she tied up?"

"No. I tried to, but she kept wiggling and kicking. Uncle Vic said we didn't get paid if she was hurt, so he locked her in the room instead."

"Paid by whom?" Alexis braced herself to hear Mara's name, but Brant shook his head.

"I don't know. Whoever hired Uncle Vic."

"Is he armed?" Zeke asked.

The young man shrugged and looked away. Zeke repeated the question. "I'm not sure," Brant admitted. "He wouldn't let me take a gun, said the person who hired him insisted. But he never goes into the wilderness without one, so he probably has one hidden somewhere. He has a hunting knife, too, and he knows how to use it." Two lines formed between the young man's eyebrows. "You don't want to cross Uncle Vic."

"Is this your uncle's cabin?" Alexis was trying to get the big picture.

"No, he worked on the crew that built it five years ago. It belongs to some guy from Silicon Valley. He only comes up in June and July, when the sockeyes are running, so Vic knew it would be empty."

Mara had done some remodeling in her house the year before. Perhaps that was where she had met this Victor person. Zeke looked at Alexis. "Any other questions for him?"

"Do you know the pilot's name?"

Brant shook his head. "No. Vic just got a message to meet at the gas pumps at Chapel Lake."

"Okay." Zeke laid a hand on Brant's shoulder. "You've been a big help, and we'll be sure the troopers know about it. In the meantime, I'm going to have to tie you to this tree." Zeke indicated a sturdy birch.

Resigned, Brant shuffled backward until he was against the tree and slid down to the ground. Zeke tied the rope around the trunk.

Alexis pulled the bandanna from her hair. "Sorry about this, but—"

"I understand." Brant opened his mouth so that she could tie the gag in place.

"We'll come back and remove that as soon as we get Keira," Alexis promised.

Zeke hid a smile, but not before Alexis caught it. Okay, maybe she shouldn't be so considerate of a kidnapper, but she got the impression Brant was something of a victim, too. Zeke motioned that she should follow him up the trail, and she nodded. It was time to make a plan. Victor was the dangerous one. They had to get Keira away from that man.

Chapter Seventeen

"We need to work fast," Zeke told Alexis as soon as they were out of earshot from the kidnapper they'd captured. "'Uncle Vic' will be expecting Brant back anytime now and I get the impression he's not the patient sort."

"Brant seems to be willing to cooperate. We could send him back in to distract Vic while we get Keira. There's a window with storm shutters on the far side. Once we unlatch the shutters, we should be able to get Keira out."

Zeke shook his head. "It's a good plan, but it would depend on Brant's ability as an actor. The impression I get is that he's more scared of his uncle than he is of us, or of law enforcement."

"Hmm, you're probably right."

"On the other hand—" Zeke rubbed his beard as he thought. "Maybe we can use that. Can you get the shutter open without creating a lot of noise?"

"I believe so. From what I saw, the shutters are latched together with a hook and eye. Nothing complicated."

"Okay, then. What if we tried this?" He outlined his plan. It was simple, but Alexis couldn't see any reason it wouldn't work. "Or," he added, "we can wait for the troopers and let them flush Vic out."

"I like your plan better," Alexis said. "If the troopers come and Vic feels cornered, he might decide to use Keira as a shield. Let's do this."

Zeke nodded. "You get in position. I'll get Brant and circle around."

Alexis silently moved to the spot behind some low bushes she'd occupied before, where she could keep an eye on the bedroom window while remaining hidden. She hoped Zeke could convince Brant to cooperate—if not, this plan could backfire big-time. But she didn't have a better one, and the sooner they could get Keira away from that man, the better. She said a quick prayer for Keira's protection.

About five minutes later, a bloodcurdling yell sounded from the forest near the porch. Heavy running footsteps pounded inside the cabin, and Poppy barked. The front door was thrown open with a bang. "Brant? What are you doing there?"

"Bear!" came the call from the woods, with much scuffling noise from the bushes. Poppy kept barking.

"Shut up, you stupid mutt." The front door slammed again. Alexis wasn't sure if Vic was inside or out, but she couldn't wait any longer.

She slipped out from her spot, raced to the window and reached for the shutters. She had to stand on her tiptoes to reach the latch but managed to unhook the shutters and lock them open. Seconds later, Keira's precious face appeared at the window. Alexis put her finger to her lips and motioned for Keira to unlock the window while she removed the screen. Keira immediately snapped the latch open.

With Alexis pushing on the outside and Keira on the inside, they jerked the window upward, but it stopped after five inches and Alexis realized someone had installed window stops. A non-opening bedroom window had to be against building codes, but since there was no building inspector handy, she supposed they'd have to work with it. She pointed at the wing nuts. "Unscrew them," she whispered through the opening at the bottom of the window.

Keira tried, but the screws seemed to be stuck. Meanwhile, Alexis could hear more thrashing in the bushes, with Brant hollering something about looking for a tree to climb. "I can't get them," Keira hissed.

Alexis pushed her arms through the opening, but she couldn't get her hands on the screws. "Can you get out the back way?"

Keira shook her head. "I'm locked in this room."

Alexis pressed her face against the glass to peer into the room. "Okay. Here's what we're going to do. First push the desk in front of the door, but try not to make noise while you do it. Then get that blanket off the bed. Once I've closed the window again, use the chair to break as much glass out of it as you can, then throw the blanket over the bottom and get out of there."

Vic was hollering at Brant from the porch, telling him to quit being stupid and get inside, but Brant called back that the bear had him treed. Keira blocked the doorway and picked up the chair. Alexis moved away from the window.

Crash! Glass went everywhere, and the front door opened and slammed shut. Footsteps pounded down the hall. Keira used the chair to push more glass from the frame and threw the folded blanket over the bottom. Alexis helped her spread it. The doorknob rattled, but in the hallway, Poppy growled.

"Shut up, dog." Alexis heard the scratching sound of the key turning in the lock.

Keira climbed onto the nightstand and then to the window frame, avoiding the broken glass shards still clinging to the edges. The door opened a few inches, encumbered by the desk. An arm holding a pistol reached through the opening. "Stop or I'll shoot."

So much for Mara's orders. How could she have trusted her daughter to someone like Vic? Keira didn't even slow down. Victor pushed the desk back and squeezed past it into the room, with his gun pointed toward the window. "I said stop!"

Before Alexis could react, Poppy rushed into the room, leaped up and clamped her jaws onto his arm. He roared in pain. Alexis pulled Keira through the window and onto the ground. Keira stumbled, but Alexis grabbed her arm and pulled her to her feet. "Run!"

They took off into the woods. Behind them, a shot sounded from inside the cabin. Alexis gulped. *Oh, no! Poppy!* But a moment later, a blond streak raced along the game trail toward them.

"Poppy!" Keira called out.

The dog ran to her. Red blotches stained her chest, but she seemed to be moving okay. Alexis didn't have time for a closer inspection. Vic was still behind them. They kept running at top speed until they'd reached the spot with the uprooted trees Zeke had pointed out on the way in. Once the three of them were tucked in out of sight, Alexis drew Keira into a hug. "Thank God you're all right."

"Is Poppy hurt bad?"

Alexis checked. "I don't think so. The tip of her ear is bleeding a little, and it looks like she has a scrape on her shoulder from the window, but most of the blood on her chest doesn't seem to be hers. She must have done a number on that guy's arm."

"Serves him right." Keira's face was the picture of indignation. "He threw my phone in the lake."

Alexis grinned. Kidnapping and threatening her was one thing, but destroying Keira's phone was the ultimate offense. "No wonder you're mad. But now we need to be quiet."

For a long time as they sat silently, nothing happened. Eventually, they heard soft steps coming along the trail. Poppy squirmed, but Alexis held her still. Were the steps slowing? Alexis held her breath, ready, if Vic's face should suddenly appear, to fling herself at him so that Keira could run.

The familiar sound of a robin's call rang through the forest, paused and then repeated. *Zeke!* Alexis scrambled out of the hole. "We're here! All three of us!"

While Keira followed her out, Zeke ran to them and wrapped his arms around both of them. "You're okay? I didn't know what to think when I heard the breaking glass."

"The window was stuck," Keira explained. "So I had to hit it with a chair."

"Poppy? Are you hurt?" Zeke knelt and examined the dog.

"I think she'll be okay," Alexis told him. "Most of the blood is from Victor. He threatened to shoot, and Poppy bit him."

"I wondered what happened to his arm," Zeke said. "I assumed it was from the broken window."

"Is he badly injured?" Alexis asked.

"A long gash on his forearm, but it didn't catch an artery or anything." He stroked Poppy's face as he examined her wounds, which had all stopped bleeding. "Good girl. What a brave dog you are."

"So, speaking of Vic—" Alexis prompted.

Zeke stood, but kept his hand on Poppy's head. "I tackled him when he ran out the back door after you. He's tied up in a chair on the front porch, waiting for the troopers to arrive."

"And Brant?"

"He's in the woods. In return for his help in creating a diversion, I agreed to let Vic believe there really was a bear. The plan is that when the troopers come, Brant will climb down from the tree and surrender."

Keira tugged on Alexis's arm. "The guy's name is Victor?"

"That's what Brant told us."

"So it's true." Keira looked stricken.

"What is, sweetie?"

Keira answered slowly. "My mom is working with him."

Alexis had hoped to delay that revelation until Keira had a little time to recover from her experience. "What makes you say that?" she asked.

Keira looked off into the distance as she answered. "She's been acting weird. A couple times, I've seen texts and messages pop up on her phone from someone called Victor, and she always covered them up like she didn't want me to see them." She turned to Alexis. "And she canceled her cruise after you said you were taking me rafting. She said it was because she got the car and couldn't afford both, but then she complained that they hardly refunded any of the money anyway, so why would she do that?"

"We don't know anything for sure yet," Alexis cautioned.

"I do," Keira stated, flatly. "That's why I didn't

send her any of the texts from the plane. I'm even more sure now. She planned this, to get Dad to pay her money."

Zeke slipped an arm around Keira's shoulders. "It will all get sorted out. Things might be kinda rough for a while," he told her. "But remember, there are people who love you like crazy. Like your aunt, here. You can always depend on her, no matter what happens."

"Yeah." Keira nodded. "I know."

"Come with me. There's something I want to show you." Zeke led them back along the trail and up a hill to a rocky point overlooking the lake. A narrow island with three spruce trees ran parallel to the shore there. A moose stood up to her knees in the water beside the island, munching on water plants. And on the shore, playing hide-and-seek among the tall stalks of pink fireweed, were two moose calves.

"Wow." Keira laughed as one of the two frolicked and chased the other, with occasional stops to grab a bite of fireweed. "I wish I had my phone. I'd take a picture."

"You don't need a phone." Zeke laid one hand on her shoulder and the other on Alexis's. "You can remember. You'll have lots of memories, good and bad, but someone very wise told me not to let a few bad ones chase away all the good ones."

Keira managed a smile. Alexis laid her hand on top of his. "That's good advice."

Zeke winked. "I know." And they sat down to watch the moose and wait for the troopers to arrive.

Chapter Eighteen

Alexis kept her arm around Keira's thin shoulders. They stood at a distance, watching the troopers loading the handcuffed kidnappers onto a plane. The white bandage the troopers had applied to Victor's forearm stood out against his khaki shirt. Beside them, Poppy wagged her tail. All was right with her world, now that the bad guys were gone, Keira was safe and her people were together. Or maybe not. The dog was looking around, trying to figure out where Zeke had gone. At some point, he had become one of Poppy's people, too.

He'd become one of Alexis's people as well. She'd only known him a week, but she already trusted him more than anyone else in her life. If only— But she stopped that thought before it could run away with her. Zeke had made it clear, back at Chapel Lake, that he was cutting their ties. He had already done so much for her and Keira; the least Alexis could do was to let him live his chosen life without trying to extract any promises that he would be in touch. But how she wished she could. The troopers had taken him off with the excuse that they needed him to show them something on the plane they'd flown in, but Alexis suspected it was really a way to separate them so that they could get preliminary statements separately.

It was probably just as well, since Alexis didn't want to discuss Mara's likely motives for the kidnapping in front of Keira, and she wasn't about to leave her niece alone. Zeke had been the one to figure out Mara's possible involvement in the first place, so he could tell the troopers all about it. But Alexis missed his presence. It was like a pillar she had been leaning against was suddenly gone, leaving her wobbly, trying to catch her balance.

Maybe it was just shock now that the danger was finally behind them. Trooper Jane Andersen, who had interviewed them earlier, walked their way. "Keira, I've got someone on the sat phone who would like to talk with you."

Keira took the phone. "Daddy!" Alexis hadn't heard her greet her father with such enthusiasm in a long time. "Yeah, I'm okay. Did you get my texts?" Keira paced a few feet away as she talked.

Trooper Andersen smiled and nodded toward the girl. "Your niece is something, sending out those GPS coordinates like that. She is going to be a force to be reckoned with someday."

Alexis chuckled. "She already is."

"We'll need to see both of you again in Anchorage in the next day or two. Her father can come with her, of course." The trooper shifted from one foot to the other. "We haven't located her mother yet, but we will."

"I know."

Trooper Andersen touched Alexis's arm. "I'm sure you're worried, but I've seen kids like her go through much worse and come out the other side. She'll be okay. She's a strong one."

"She is. Thanks." Alexis wasn't sure what kind of strength it would take to get over the fact that your own mother arranged for you to be kidnapped by strangers, but one way or another, Keira would get through it.

Voices coming from the trail made her turn her head. Zeke and the trooper were returning. Zeke spotted her and smiled, a smile that reached all the way to her heart. He came to her and reached for her hand. "You holding up okay?"

She nodded. "I think so. Some of the troopers took off with the prisoners. Another plane should be here shortly to take us to Anchorage. Keira's talking to her dad." A blue-and-white floatplane came into view and dropped onto the lake. "In fact, there's our ride."

"Right. Well, I suppose I should return my friend's plane to Chapel Lake before the troopers decide to arrest me for grand theft."

"Zeke, I don't know how to thank you—"

"You don't need to. Come here." He pulled her into a hug. "It's all going to be okay."

"Zeke!" Keira handed the phone back to the trooper and ran over for a hug of her own.

"Hey, there." He tilted up Keira's chin so that he could look into her eyes. "You're going to rock middle school, Tejónita. You know that, right?"

Keira nodded and gave him a watery smile.

"Good. Okay, then. You two take care. *Vaya con Dios.*"

"To you as well," Alexis answered.

"What does that mean?" Keira leaned against Alexis as they watched Zeke walk away.

Alexis squeezed Keira's shoulders. "'Go with God.'"

Chapter Nineteen

〜

"Got your lunch? Don't forget your homework." Alexis scooped up the math assignment Keira had left on the kitchen island and handed it to her.

Keira stuffed it into her backpack. "Thanks."

Dressed in the Seahawks pajamas Keira had given him last Christmas, Dixon leaned against the island and checked the calendar on his phone. "Rachel is driving you, Sarah and Elise from school to soccer practice this afternoon. I'll be picking up." Dixon handed his daughter a jacket and planted a kiss on the top of her head. "We can all go for pizza if you want."

"Great! I'll text Elise and Sarah." Keira reached for her cell phone, a duplicate of the one she'd carried on the raft trip.

"Right now, you'd better go or you'll miss the bus," Dixon pointed out.

Keira nodded and walked toward the door, but she continued to text. Just before she stepped outside, she pocketed her phone and shot him a grin. "Thanks, Dad. See you after practice."

Dixon moved to the window, where he hovered near the curtain, trying to be inconspicuous as he watched Keira join the other kids at the bus stop. Alexis knew he wouldn't budge from that spot until Keira was safely on the bus. After all that had happened, Alexis didn't much blame him. She poured a second cup of coffee and brought it to him. "Pizza. Nice."

"Thanks." He accepted the coffee. "I figure hanging around while she spends time with her friends might be a good way to get to know my daughter better."

"For sure." Alexis patted her brother's shoulder. "You're doing well. Keira can see that you're trying."

He shook his head. "I can hardly believe it came to this. That Mara was so resentful after the divorce she would literally hold Keira hostage, and that I was oblivious to it all. When I got that text from Keira saying she'd been kidnapped, I was terrified. And I realized I've been spending too much time on the wrong things." He sipped his coffee and watched his daughter board the bus. Without turning his head, he said, "They arrested Mara this morning. She was trying to cross the border to Canada with a forged passport."

"I see." It was only a matter of time. Once Victor was in custody, he'd been only too eager to blame everything on Mara. According to Victor, he and

Mara had been having an affair for the past year, and she'd seduced him into helping her with the kidnapping, promising they would live together someplace tropical once she had the money. Alexis suspected Mara's lawyer would tell a different story, but it didn't matter. They would all be going to prison.

"It will probably hit the news later today," Dixon continued. "Do you think Keira will be okay?"

"I do. It's going to be hard for a while, but we'll try to keep her life as routine as possible. The therapist says she's doing well, and she seems to be adjusting to middle school. I'm sure there will be a few bumps, but that's always the case when you're dealing with teenagers."

"Teenager." Dixon shook his head in wonder. "How can she be turning thirteen in a month? She was just a baby, like, ten minutes ago."

"It seems like it."

"Birthday." His eyes widened. "I'm going to need your help planning a party. What do thirteen-year-olds like, anyway? Is it cake and pony rides, or a formal ball?"

Alexis laughed. "Somewhere in between, I'd imagine. Your best bet is to ask her. Keira has no problem articulating what she wants."

"True, but I don't want to overdo it. Maybe I'll ask Sarah's mom what she thinks."

"Good idea." Alexis had been noticing a growing friendship between Sarah's mother, Rachel, and Dixon. Now that Dixon was Keira's full-time parent,

Rachel, who had lost her husband when Sarah was a preschooler, had been a wonderful source of advice and encouragement. Alexis knew and liked Rachel from her involvement at their church, and hoped the relationship might bloom into something more, but that was up to them. She set her cup in the dishwasher. "I'd better head home. Lots of work waiting."

"I appreciate you staying with us all this time. It's been a big help."

"No problem. But I plan to move out this weekend. Keira's feeling secure here with you now. She doesn't need me around 24/7."

"But you'll still spend time with her?"

"Of course. I'll call every day, and I'll see her several times a week. And you can always call me if you need me to drive carpool or anything."

"I'll do that. Come here." He pulled Alexis into a hug. "Thank you for bringing my daughter back to me."

Alexis turned in at the entryway to her neighborhood and then onto her own lane and pulled up at the stop sign to wait for another car to pass. Down the block, she could see Mr. Vang, her retired neighbor across the street, out mowing his lawn with an old-fashioned reel-type push mower. Mr. Vang was a big believer in the tried and true over cutting edge. Too bad he couldn't meet Zeke and watch him work on his cabin. They would have a lot to talk about.

Zeke. She'd assumed that as time went by, she

would stop thinking about him every minute, but the more days that passed, the more he seemed to be on her mind. Did he make it home? Did the kidnappers do any damage to his home or the site? Did he worry about Keira and her the way she worried about him? It was so frustrating not to be able to call him, just to check if he was okay. She shook her head. No use fooling herself. A call wouldn't be enough. She wanted to see him, to touch his face, to put her arms around him and hold him. Was it possible he was out there, wishing for the same thing?

The car went by and she pulled forward and turned into her driveway. Her own lawn had been freshly cut. She smiled at Mr. Vang across the street. So sweet of him. Not that she couldn't mow her own lawn, but she knew this was her neighbor's way of letting her know he cared. She made a mental note to invite him and his whole extended family over for a barbecue along with Dixon and Keira one day soon.

She was about to punch the button for the garage door when she noticed a man getting up from the deep red Adirondack chair on her front porch. Her heart beat faster. She wasn't expecting any clients today. Instead of opening the garage, she got out of her car and made a point of calling good morning to Mr. Vang, so that whoever was on the porch would realize there was a witness. Everything was probably fine, but she had to be careful. She hated the way this kidnapping and the publicity around it had made her afraid in her own neighborhood.

Poppy jumped out of the car and must have sensed her discomfort, because she positioned herself between Alexis and the house. The man on the porch took a step closer, moving from the shade to the sun. He had dark hair, cut short, and a very strange-looking pale beard. Suddenly, Poppy was wagging her tail. The man's face broke into a familiar grin, and Alexis realized it wasn't a beard at all, but skin that had been hidden under a beard and never exposed to the sun. "Zeke!"

He opened his arms, and she ran into them, laughing, as she threw her arms around his neck. "I was just thinking about you."

He pulled her close and held her as if he couldn't get enough. He smelled of soap and a spicy after-shave. "I haven't been able to stop thinking about you." Poppy woofed and jumped with excitement, and Zeke laid a hand on the dog's head.

Zeke was here! Alexis tried not to read too much into that, but she couldn't help but hope. Without letting him go, she drew back just enough so that she could look into his face, at the kind brown eyes she knew so well and the strong jawline that had been hiding under that beard. "How did you get here?"

"Well." He grinned. "I tried to run, but there was this big fish…"

"And he swallowed you and took you all the way down the Pearson River to the ocean, up Cook Inlet, past Fire Island, and then followed Campbell Creek to my neighborhood and dropped you here?"

"Something like that."

She laughed. "You look pretty good for a man who's been living inside a fish."

He chuckled. "Well, I did stop for a shave and haircut along the way."

"I see that. I like the new look." She caressed his smooth cheek. "Or I will once you get a little more sun."

Mr. Vang had crossed the street and stood in her yard. "So, all is okay here?"

Alexis turned. "Yes, more than okay, thank you. Zeke Soto, this is my wonderful neighbor, Mr. Vang, who I suspect mowed my lawn this morning. Thank you so much."

Mr. Vang waved away her thanks and shook hands with Zeke. Satisfied that she was safe, he went back to his mowing. Alexis took Zeke's hand. "Come inside."

"I like your house," he told her, looking up at the carved beams that supported the cedar-lined porch roof. She clicked the fob that disarmed the security system and unlocked the front door.

"Thanks." They stepped into the sunroom, which had a door at each end, one marked with her office logo, and the other that led into her living space. A different button on the fob unlocked that door and she ushered him into her great room. Poppy flopped down on her dog bed next to the sliding glass door. "Delta, morning mode, summer." Indirect overhead lighting and a stained-glass lamp on the end table beside the couch switched on. Soft but cheerful instrumental music mixed with birdsong played in the background. Windows looking out toward the backyard slid open a few inches to allow fresh air inside.

"Wow. What happens in winter morning mode?"

"More lights, and instead of opening the windows, it lights the fireplace."

"Impressive." Zeke looked around the living room at the Craftsman-style furniture and built-in entertainment system. "A little different living here than in the log cabin. Is that coffee I smell?"

"It is." She'd already activated the coffee maker when she turned into the neighborhood. "I love my house, but your cabin holds a special place in my heart. Have a seat. I'll get us coffee." She filled two mugs and put them on a tray, along with a plate of oatmeal cookies she'd picked up the day before from a bake sale at church. After setting the tray on the live-edge table in front of the couch, she sat down beside him and smiled. "I can't get over how different you look without a beard."

"Hopefully, the tan line won't scare my clients too much until I can make my face match."

"Clients? Does that mean—"

"Yes. I found a job in the physical rehab department at one of the hospitals here in Anchorage." He reached for her hands. "You were right. I told myself I was doing the right thing living out there in the woods alone, but really, I was running from God. From asking for forgiveness. Because as long as I was unforgiven, I didn't have to worry that God would ask anything of me. I didn't have to worry about failing someone again. But then you and Keira showed up."

"And you helped us. Even though you didn't know us, you took us in and protected us."

He nodded. "And I discovered that I can still care. That I can still love. If God is willing to forgive me, I should be able to forgive myself. I know that Dani is with God, and that she would want me to go on and live the life God meant for me to live."

"Yes."

"And that's why I'm here." He swallowed. "I don't want to presume, but if you're willing, I'd very much like for you to be a part of that life."

"Oh, Zeke." Alexis blinked back the tears that were forming in her eyes. "You can't imagine how happy I am to hear that."

"I think I can." And then he was kissing her, and it felt so right. Whether it was here in Anchorage, or in a rustic cabin in the wilderness, or even on a patch-work raft, this was where they belonged. Together.

Epilogue

One Year Later

"Everything is just lovely." Zeke's aunt Linda, all dressed up in pink lace, beamed up at him. With Alexis's encouragement, he'd renewed his relationships with his aunts, uncles and cousins, and several of them had traveled to Alaska for the festivities. She patted his cheek. "You did good. Your mother would absolutely adore your new wife."

His new wife. Despite having looked into Alexis's eyes and vowed to love and honor her always, Zeke still found it hard to believe that Alexis was actually his wife. That this amazing woman had agreed to spend her life with him. Aunt Linda was right—Mom would have adored Alexis. They were a lot alike, both strong women who believed in family and in God. Who celebrated the beauty of the world and who treated people with love and kindness. Zeke wished his mother could be here, but he had the feeling that, somehow, she was. His eyes searched for Alexis, there on the other side of the room, her eyes merry as she listened to some story his uncle was telling.

He always found Alexis beautiful, but today, in her long white dress with her glossy hair pinned up with flowers, she took his breath away. Her brother had offered to pay for any kind of wedding her heart desired, but she said she didn't want a lot of fuss. Instead, she'd chosen a simple ceremony and reception here at the church where she had belonged all her life and where Zeke had made so many friends over the past year. All of whom were gathered here in this room, along with coworkers and family members, to celebrate with them.

"Zeke? Ezekiel!" Aunt Linda's voice called him back.

"Sorry. I was—"

"Staring at your beautiful bride." She laughed. "I understand. Why don't you go to her now?"

"I will." Zeke kissed his aunt's cheek before crossing the room to stand beside Alexis. While still listening to Uncle Joe, she reached for Zeke's hand and squeezed. He looked down at the rings on her finger, the diamond engagement ring he had given her on New Year's Eve and the wedding band that symbolized their never-ending love. He didn't deserve a woman like Alexis, but she loved him from dawn till dusk, a miracle for which Zeke would be forever grateful.

Poppy wandered over and leaned against Zeke's leg while he scratched her ears. As one of the official attendants, she wore a collar of pink peonies that matched the ones in Alexis's and Keira's bouquets.

"…and then Zeke asked, 'Why were the shepherds' socks so dirty?'" Uncle Joe finished his story with a flourish, and everyone laughed, especially Keira. Zeke and Alexis traded smiles.

Zeke had told her that story of misunderstood lyrics last Christmas when they'd sung the hymn together. Alexis admitted she had also heard "shepherds washed their socks," instead of "watched their flocks," and for a time she'd assumed that was where the tradition of Christmas stockings had come from. Later Zeke had shopped until he found some miniature stockings and a tiny washtub intended for dollhouses. He'd slipped them in among the shepherds in Alexis's nativity scene when she wasn't looking. When she discovered them later, she'd laughed so hard she got the hiccups. He could hardly wait to celebrate next Christmas as a married couple.

"Time to cut the cake," someone called, and everyone gathered around while Zeke and Alexis fed one another the first bites of the chocolate-and-raspberry swirl cake baked by Rachel, the mother of Keira's good friend Sarah. Once they'd had their taste, Rachel stepped forward to cut slices for the guests, but not before Alexis had given her a grateful hug.

Recently, Rachel and Dixon had begun to date seriously, and Alexis was overjoyed, already looking forward to the day when Rachel might become Keira's stepmother. Rachel's experience as a single parent had been a huge help to Dixon in the past year. Zeke had to hand it to the man. He still ran Mahoney Tours, but after Keira's kidnapping, Dixon had made the decision to put his daughter and his faith first, and he'd stuck to that commitment to the point where Zeke had trouble imagining the business-obsessed man Alexis had once described.

While people were waiting for their cake, Dixon approached Zeke and Alexis. He gave his sister a hug and then stepped back to admire her. "You look just like Mom, in their wedding picture."

"Aw, thank you." Alexis beamed. "She was beautiful."

"So are you." Dixon gave Zeke a fierce stare that would have worried him if he hadn't gotten to know Dixon well enough over the last year to know when he was kidding. "You'd better be good to my sister."

"I'll do my very best," Zeke promised and accepted a one-armed hug from his new brother-in-law.

Keira joined them as Dixon asked, "So where are you going on your honeymoon? I heard something about Belize, or possibly Kauai? Keira and I will be happy to dog-sit for you."

"Thanks, but we won't need a dogsitter," Alexis answered. She smiled up at Zeke as he put an arm around her waist. "We were considering both those places but—"

"I'll bet I know where," Keira broke in.

Alexis seemed amused at the smug look on her niece's face. "Let's hear your guess."

"I think you're going back to the Pearson River to finish building the cabin. Am I right?"

"You are indeed," Zeke confirmed.

Dixon's eyebrows drew together and he studied Alexis's face. "I'd have thought that place might bring back some bad memories for you."

"No," Alexis assured him and leaned her head on Zeke's shoulder. "Despite everything, I always felt safe there in the cabin with Zeke, even in the middle of a storm. It will always be a special place for us. That cabin is where God brought us together."

Zeke kissed the top of her head. "It's the place we fell in love."

* * * * *

LOVE INSPIRED

Stories to uplift and inspire

Fall in love with Love Inspired—
inspirational and uplifting stories of faith
and hope. Find strength and comfort in
the bonds of friendship and community.
Revel in the warmth of possibility and the
promise of new beginnings.

Sign up for the Love Inspired newsletter
at **LoveInspired.com** to be the first
to find out about upcoming titles,
special promotions and exclusive content.

CONNECT WITH US AT:

f Facebook.com/LoveInspiredBooks

🐦 Twitter.com/LoveInspiredBks

Get 4 FREE REWARDS!

We'll send you 2 FREE Books plus 2 FREE Mystery Gifts.

FREE
Value Over
$20

Both the **Love Inspired®** and **Love Inspired® Suspense** series feature compelling
novels filled with inspirational romance, faith, forgiveness, and hope.

YES! Please send me 2 FREE novels from the Love Inspired or Love Inspired
Suspense series and my 2 FREE gifts (gifts are worth about $10 retail). After
receiving them, if I don't wish to receive any more books, I can return the shipping
statement marked "cancel." If I don't cancel, I will receive 6 brand-new Love Inspired
Larger-Print books or Love Inspired Suspense Larger-Print books every month and
be billed just $6.24 each in the U.S. or $6.49 each in Canada. That is a savings of at
least 17% off the cover price. It's quite a bargain! Shipping and handling is just 50¢
per book in the U.S. and $1.25 per book in Canada.* I understand that accepting the
2 free books and gifts places me under no obligation to buy anything. I can always
return a shipment and cancel at any time by calling the number below. The free
books and gifts are mine to keep no matter what I decide.

Choose one: ☐ **Love Inspired**
    Larger-Print
    (122/322 IDN GRDF)

☐ **Love Inspired Suspense**
    Larger-Print
    (107/307 IDN GRDF)

Name (please print)

Address   Apt. #

City   State/Province   Zip/Postal Code

Email: Please check this box ☐ if you would like to receive newsletters and promotional emails from Harlequin Enterprises ULC and
its affiliates. You can unsubscribe anytime.

Mail to the **Harlequin Reader Service:**
IN U.S.A.: P.O. Box 1341, Buffalo, NY 14240-8531
IN CANADA: P.O. Box 603, Fort Erie, Ontario L2A 5X3

Want to try 2 free books from another series! Call 1-800-873-8635 or visit www.ReaderService.com.

*Terms and prices subject to change without notice. Prices do not include sales taxes, which will be charged (if applicable) based
on your state or country of residence. Canadian residents will be charged applicable taxes. Offer not valid in Quebec. This offer is
limited to one order per household. Books received may not be as shown. Not valid for current subscribers to the Love Inspired or
Love Inspired Suspense series. All orders subject to approval. Credit or debit balances in a customer's account(s) may be offset by
any other outstanding balance owed by or to the customer. Please allow 4 to 6 weeks for delivery. Offer available while quantities last.

Your Privacy—Your information is being collected by Harlequin Enterprises ULC, operating as Harlequin Reader Service. For a
complete summary of the information we collect, how we use this information and to whom it is disclosed, please visit our privacy notice
located at corporate.harlequin.com/privacy-notice. From time to time we may also exchange your personal information with reputable
third parties. If you wish to opt out of this sharing of your personal information, please visit readerservice.com/consumerchoice or
call 1-800-873-8635. **Notice to California Residents**—Under California law, you have specific rights to control and access your data.
For more information on these rights and how to exercise them, visit corporate.harlequin.com/california-privacy.

LIRLIS22R2

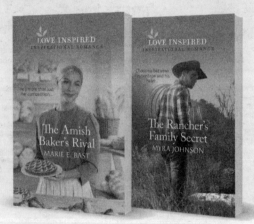